The doll was smashed.

Becky looked at the head. It was a thousand little pieces, yet the body was whole, lying like a miniature abandoned child.

One painted blue eye stared at Becky, accusingly.

"It's him," Mrs. Nelson said, her face white and her eyes staring blankly at the shattered doll.

"He's here. He's found us."

Also in the Point Horror series:

April Fools
The Lifeguard
Teacher's Pet
Trick or Treat
by Richie Tankersley Cusick

My Secret Admirer
by Carol Ellis

Funhouse
The Invitation
by Diane Hoh

Thirteen
by Christopher Pike, R. L. Stine and others

Beach Party
The Baby-sitter
The Baby-sitter II
The Boyfriend
The Girlfriend
The Snowman
by R. L. Stine

Look out for:

The Accident
by Diane Hoh

The Cheerleader
by Caroline B. Cooney

The Return of the Vampire
by Caroline B. Cooney

The Window
by Carol Ellis

Point Horror

MOTHER'S HELPER

A. Bates

Hippo Books
Scholastic Children's Books
London

Scholastic Children's Books
Scholastic Publications Ltd,
7-9 Pratt Street, London NW1 0AE, UK

Scholastic Inc.,
730 Broadway, New York, NY 10003, USA

Scholastic Canada Ltd,
123 Newkirk Road, Richmond Hill,
Ontario Canada, L4C 3G5

Ashton Scholastic Pty Ltd,
P O Box 579, Gosford, New South Wales,
Australia

Ashton Scholastic Ltd,
Private Bag 1, Penrose, Auckland
New Zealand

First published in the US by Scholastic Inc., 1991
First published in the UK by Scholastic Publications Ltd, 1992

Copyright © Auline Bates, 1991

ISBN 0 590 55059 4

Printed by Cox & Wyman Ltd, Reading, Berks

10 9 8

All rights reserved

*There have been many good people in my life —
people who made me want to try harder, do a better
job, be a better human being. This book is
dedicated to two of those people: Mark Shaw,
teacher, and Greg Holch, editor.*

Thank you.

MOTHER'S HELPER

Chapter 1

Becky Collier listened for the baby as she rolled her shorts up and moved her towel farther into the sunshine.

What a way to earn expenses for college next year, she thought, closing her eyes against the sun. Working as a mother's helper on a romantic island . . . one well-behaved little boy to watch, a little housework, time to work on my tan. I've got it made.

Just think, she reminded herself smugly. I could be fogbound in Seattle at this very moment, flipping burgers and grilling special orders. She made a face. And watching Jason flirt with my best friend.

Ex-best friend, she amended. Best friends don't take guys away from each other . . . not that Jason screamed in protest.

The trees towered around her, silent and grim, the shadows green and mysterious. But the sun was gently warm and hypnotic, teasing her toward sleep. Becky could feel herself growing drowsy, so she rolled over and forced herself to stand up, stretching. She crossed the twenty feet to the cabin and peeked in Devon's window.

He was curled up in his crib, his eyes closed, the middle two fingers of his right hand just slipping out of his mouth.

Satisfied that he was napping peacefully, Becky resumed her spot on the towel. She rolled her T-shirt up, pulling the front up through the neck, tugging it snug, transforming the loose T-shirt into a halter top. Then she closed her eyes again, relaxing, but alert for any sound from Devon's room.

The sudden crackle of twigs breaking didn't come from the direction of the baby's room, but Becky's eyes flew open anyway. Twigs only broke when stepped on, and no one was supposed to be around, stepping on things.

She leapt to her feet, pulling quickly on the front of her T-shirt, yanking her handiwork loose. She didn't see anyone, but there weren't any animals on the island, so it had to be a person.

Someone was near.

The silence and shadows seemed suddenly alive, vaguely threatening, and Becky was keenly aware that the nearest neighbor was half a mile downhill through the forest.

Too far away to hear if she called for help.

Chapter 2

Becky glanced around, her heart pounding loudly. The snapping of twigs sounded again, to her right, and she whirled.

The guy who emerged from the trees looked seventeen or eighteen. He had curly brown hair, kind of long, and was dressed in the faded, ragged jeans and sturdy boots the locals wore.

"Who are you?" Becky asked abruptly, embarrassed that he'd seen her hastily rearrange her clothes, and slightly uneasy at seeing a stranger suddenly appear in front of her. She glanced nervously towards Devon's window.

"Cleve Davidson," he said, frowning. "I came . . . where's John Hillyer?"

Becky had the odd feeling Cleve had been standing in the woods for some time, concealed, watching her. The thought made her uncomfortable, especially since that meant he'd seen her look in Devon's window. "Mr. Hillyer rented the cabin," she said shortly. "To us."

Mrs. Nelson had explained the island's reputation when she'd interviewed Becky for the job. "It's a little island called Sebastian," she'd said. "It's isolated — a place for people who want to get away. That's why I chose it. No one will ask questions. No one will pry."

Wrong, Becky thought. Someone is prying. He may not be asking questions, but he was spying on me. I know he was.

"Who all's living here, anyway?" Cleve asked.

"Just me and my aunt," Becky said quickly, hoping the lie didn't sound like one. Now he's asking questions, too, she thought. Prying. And it's time for Devon to get up. I've got to get this guy to leave.

"Nice hair," Cleve said.

Becky reached behind her back, pulling aside a handful of honey-brown hair. "Thanks," she said uneasily. People often commented on her hair. It was long enough to sit on, and she'd always enjoyed the friendly attention it brought her. But she wasn't sure she wanted friendly attention from Cleve.

"Have you ever cut it?" he asked.

Becky shook her head. For some reason, his question made her think of knives and the old movie where Jack Nicholson went insane in a remote, forest-surrounded resort.

Kind of like this place, she thought, glancing quickly around.

"It reminds me of Rapunzel," Cleve said.

I'm not sure that was a happy-ever-after story, Becky thought, edging towards her towel. She picked it up.

"I always liked fairy tales," Cleve said.

They always scared me, Becky thought, folding her towel, wishing he would leave and quit asking questions. The king always offered a wonderful reward — usually his daughter — but whoever failed in the quest was put to death.

"Have you been here long?" he asked.

Becky picked up her sunscreen and her book, hoping he would take the hint. "Three and a half days," she said. "And I love it. Especially the sunshine."

"How do you like being alone?"

Becky frowned uneasily at the undertones in the question.

People came to Sebastian Island for solitude, so supposedly, she was here because she wanted to be alone. Of course, it wasn't Becky, but her employer, who wanted the privacy, but Cleve couldn't know that. And to tell the truth, Becky admitted silently, all this being alone gets a bit wearing. The baby is sweet, but Mrs. Nelson gets on my nerves for some reason.

"It's perfect," she said. "Just what I wanted this summer."

"A lot of people come here to be alone," Cleve said, "and find they don't like it. It's not that easy getting off this island. You have to wait for a ferry, unless you have your own boat."

He paused, looking around. Becky couldn't read his face. "I just happen to have my own boat," he added.

Becky shuddered. The ride over on the ferry hadn't been too bad, but ferries were big. Their size made them seem safe. Regular boats were very small and didn't offer much protection from an entire ocean. I'll skip the boat ride, she thought.

"I guess I'd better be going," Cleve said. "Look me up when you come to town. South End isn't very big, but it is a tourist-oriented town. There's lots to do. Maybe I could take you out for a sail in my boat." He headed back towards the trees.

Becky headed for the cabin. That was a strange encounter, she thought. I wonder if all the locals are that . . . colorful.

"Don't forget the boat ride!" Cleve called after her.

Becky shivered. I wouldn't mind a boat ride, she thought, if it didn't mean being on all that water. Swimming isn't my strongest skill! But I would like to get into town. I would like a break from Mrs. Nelson. I wonder when my days off are? I don't remember discussing time off.

She sighed, looking around at the magnificent fir trees and the rugged hillsides. It doesn't look that different from Seattle, she thought. But there's something about being on an island . . . it's different, somehow. Cleve had a point. It's because I can't get away. Islands are hard to escape from. It makes me feel a little bit like a prisoner. And if something went wrong, I'd really be stuck!

She shivered, suddenly feeling very alone and very far from her family. Don't be silly, she told herself. What could go wrong?

Chapter 3

Ten days, Becky thought glumly. Ten days since I've seen anyone but Devon and Mrs. Nelson . . . and Cleve, one time. Unless I imagined him. I think I imagined him.

She handed Devon a pan and a wooden spoon to play with, and he banged happily, his face intent, while she worked on dinner.

The San Juan Islands, she thought, checking the rolls in the oven. A little spot of sunshine off the Washington coast. Okay, I admit every time we went for a drive in the mountains I would look down at the Islands and wish I were there instead of in the mist and the rain. I admit the scenery is spectacular, and the sun is almost always shining. But now that I've memorized every tree within Devon-hearing distance of the cabin . . .

Becky double-checked the menu Mrs. Nelson had written up. Chicken salad, rolls. Sweet potatoes, Toddler Chicken Dinner, applesauce.

The last three items were jars of baby food to be

opened for Devon. Becky warmed the sweet potatoes and Toddler Chicken Dinner in Devon's new
Bugs Bunny "heat and serve" baby dish, then trans-
ferred the removable "keep-warm" bowls to his new
high chair.

Everything Devon had was new. A lot of his
clothing had still had the tags on when she'd arrived,
and Becky had thought it strange. Becky always
felt slightly guilty using his things, aware that
every time she touched them, they became less
new, and more used. She'd noticed the almost-
wistful way her boss touched the new little shirts
and blankets, how she ran her hand across the pad-
ded sides of the new playpen, or sometimes hugged
the new stuffed animals.

Almost as if the new things mean more than the
old baby, Becky thought, tossing the salad with oil
and vinegar. She doesn't touch and hug and cuddle
him as much as she does his things.

That isn't fair, she told herself as she called her
boss to dinner. She loves her son. She's probably
just not used to being around him so much. Rich
people don't take care of their kids — they hire nan-
nies. It must be a shock to her to realize babies get
dirty and cry and make a lot of noise.

She took the pan and the spoon away from Devon
and plunked him in his high chair, snapping a new
bib around his neck.

Mrs. Nelson fed her son his sweet potatoes, then,
as usual when he got too cranky, she turned the job
over to Becky.

"He's such a fussy eater," Mrs. Nelson said.

Becky just smiled. She said the same thing every night.

He wouldn't be a fussy eater if you'd let him feed himself, Becky thought.

She stifled a sigh. After ten days, she still wasn't sure if she liked her boss. There was something about her that bothered Becky, even though she couldn't have said exactly what it was.

Mrs. Nelson was trim and well-dressed, her dark hair in a sleek cut. She was pleasant enough, except for the underlying tension. And that was understandable.

But she's not a warm person, Becky thought, singing softly to Devon to distract him from grabbing the spoon. She just doesn't understand babies, that's all.

"He's so fussy this time of day," Mrs. Nelson said.

Becky remembered the schedule Mrs. Nelson had given her the first day. Every minute of Devon's day was planned, including whether he could play on the floor or in the playpen, what time he could eat and sleep, and when he was to have his diaper changed.

Becky, surprised, had said, "What happens if his diaper is dirty before eleven-fifteen?"

Mrs. Nelson had grown icily polite. "Unscheduled people lack discipline, and discipline begins in the cradle," she'd informed Becky. "He will learn to do what he's taught to do."

Becky didn't dare suggest that Devon should be allowed to feed himself now, or that he was old enough to be eating table food. She just went on feeding him in spite of his protests and tried to drum up the courage to mention time off.

As Devon's fussing grew more determined, Becky absently handed him her own spoon, and delighted, he started banging the metal tray of his high chair.

"He has quieter toys," Mrs. Nelson commented, her expression pained. "Which he does *not* play with at the dinner table."

"Sorry," Becky said. "I think he's going to be a musician. He has a great sense of rhythm."

Devon quit banging the tray and stuck the spoon in the bowl of applesauce.

That's your dessert, Becky thought wryly. You'll get in trouble for eating dessert first, and for eating by yourself before your schedule says you may.

Mrs. Nelson was busy eating and not looking at her son, but Becky knew it would only be a minute or two before she glanced up. Will she get mad? Becky wondered. Or just sickeningly polite? Either way she'll be tense all evening and Devon will get crabby.

Becky leaned toward Mrs. Nelson, half-blocking her view of her son. "I understand there's a lot to do in town," Becky said, hoping to distract Mrs. Nelson's attention from Devon, as well as lead her into a discussion of a few hours off.

To her side, she could see Devon stick the

applesauce-coated spoon in his mouth.

"Oh?" Mrs. Nelson made it a question. "How did you come to understand this? I didn't know you'd talked with anyone."

Oops, Becky thought. I never mentioned Cleve. "Remember when Mr. Hillyer picked me up?" she asked quickly. "From the ferry? On the drive up he told me what some of the buildings were, and we talked about some of the things going on in town."

All true, Becky thought defensively. We did.

Mrs. Nelson relaxed, and Becky frowned. Why did she hire me if she doesn't trust me? she thought. I wouldn't endanger Devon.

"It looked like a fun little town," Becky went on. "I'd like to look around and go shopping."

Mrs. Nelson tensed up again. Becky tallied the signals mentally — the knuckles tightened around the water glass, the lips pale and compressed, the muscle along the jawline jumping in little pulses like a heartbeat.

She's really upset, Becky thought, disappointed. Why? All I want to do is go into town. If she trusts me to watch her son all summer, why can't she trust me to keep my mouth shut in town?

"Devon is a darling," Becky said firmly. "I care about him as if he were one of my little brothers. I would never do anything to hurt him. I would never mention him, not to anyone. But I need some time off and I want to spend it in town."

"You're not happy here."

Becky looked up sharply, surprised. Mrs. Nelson

had never asked her how she was doing, or mentioned feelings, or worried about Becky being happy. "Of course I am," she said. "It's just that once Devon's asleep there's not much to do. I've written everybody long letters about how beautiful this place is, and now there's nothing left to say. It's awfully quiet around here after Devon's bedtime. Even you don't stay here much."

Mrs. Nelson actually looked half-sympathetic, and Becky crossed her fingers under the table.

"You don't know anyone in town, do you?" Mrs. Nelson asked.

"No," Becky said. I don't actually know Cleve, she thought. I met him once. Talked with him a few minutes. That's all.

"What would you do in town if you didn't know anyone?"

"I'd be a perfect little tourist," Becky said. "Go shopping, look at the coastline, wander through town, try a coffee shop."

Devon had finished eating, so he dropped his spoon on the floor. He chuckled, looking down at it.

Becky got a warm cloth, then twisted her napkin into a ball with long ears. She hopped the napkin-bunny across the baby's tray while she washed his face and hands with the cloth.

Mrs. Nelson watched, looking oddly sad. "You seem to have a way with children," she said.

"That's one good thing about having three little brothers," Becky told her, wrapping Devon's pacifier in the napkin so he wouldn't see it and demand it. He was supposed to be giving it up. "Maybe the only good thing. I've put in more hours of my life baby-sitting than anything else. Even shopping." She took a rubber band from the counter and wrapped it around the napkin.

Mrs. Nelson smiled slowly. "I guess we could give it a try," she said. "You can go to town tonight. We'll see how it goes. But be careful."

Chapter 4

The woods were almost-dark and shadowy. Becky hefted the flashlight and shone it on the path, wondering exactly how far it was into town.

Two miles? Or did Mrs. Nelson say one mile? Whatever it is, it's mostly downhill, which means mostly uphill coming back. But she needs to have the car. I guess I didn't really expect her to offer it to me. Two miles in the dark is not that far. And anyway, it's not that dark.

She wondered if there were any snakes.

They could be slithering around all over, she thought, listening for rustles in the undergrowth. But they don't slither at night, do they? Don't they need the sun or something?

She looked around warily, suddenly remembering there were more things than snakes to worry about. I don't need to be afraid, she reminded herself. This isn't Seattle. This is a small island, where everybody knows everybody. Walking in the woods here is not like walking alone in a city. It's safe.

She jumped, startled, when she saw another light shimmering through the trees. "Hello?" she called.

"Rapunzel?" she heard.

"Cleve!" she said. What's he doing out here at night?

"I saw your light," he called, as if guessing her question.

His voice carried clearly through the night air, and Becky hoped they were too far from her cabin for Mrs. Nelson to hear. I'm not supposed to talk to anyone, she thought guiltily. I'm not supposed to know anyone.

Becky could hear his footfalls, now, thudding in the depths of the woods. She had a sudden impulse to run from him, but fought it back. She was too lonely for company to run from him, even if he was a little strange.

"Yours is the last cabin up this way," Cleve said, his voice floating through the forest. "So when I saw the light, I figured it was you. Your aunt always uses the car."

Cleve and his light joined her. "So I said to myself, look, a maiden. Rescue her. Do you need rescuing?"

"Actually, I've never needed rescuing in my whole life," Becky told him, joining him warily. They set off together down the hill. "In fact, I'm the one who rescues everyone else. One of my little brothers almost drowned — in a wading pool, no less — but I rescued him." She shivered at the memory.

"Isn't it kind of hard to drown in a wading pool?" Cleve asked.

"No," Becky said. "It doesn't take much water at all for little guys to drown in." And if it had been a real pool, I couldn't have saved him, she thought. I'd have tried, but we'd have both drowned. I can float. I can do a back float with a kick. I can't swim.

They walked in silence for a moment, and then Cleve said, "Watch it, here. There's a big rut."

They maneuvered around the rut and hiked on, Becky wondering about Cleve. The way he saw the light right away, he had to be watching for something, she thought. Me? Is he watching me that closely? But why would he do that?

She felt uneasy still, especially since Cleve didn't say anything else. Why is he here? she kept wondering. But after awhile, his presence was oddly comforting. It was nicer to walk through strange woods with someone who knew the path.

She was surprised to notice how close the lights of town were already. She and Cleve had hardly said anything to each other, and still the walk had gone quickly.

"Would you like to go for a moonlight sail?" Cleve asked suddenly.

Not on your life, Becky thought. Just you, me, a little boat, and all that dark water? Uh-uh! "No thanks," she said. "I plan on shopping and going to the library for some books."

"Via the ice-cream shop," Cleve said, pointing.

They'd reached the edge of town and switched off their lights.

"Should I tell you your story?" he asked, opening the door to a small, bright shop. "I've had a week to make one up."

"I'm listening," Becky said. "I always wanted to know the story of my life. '*The Absolute Best Dessert Establishment*,' " she read above the door. "Is that true?"

"Absolutely. This place is six blocks from my uncle's house, and I discovered it the summer I was six. I realized it was an omen that the numbers matched. Six and six. I like omens."

He makes the strangest comments, Becky thought. She chose a chocolate fudge cone, and Cleve had strawberries and cream. They wandered down South End's main business street, enjoying their cones.

"It's certainly the best ice cream I've ever had," Becky told him.

"And since you're rich, you're used to having only the best," Cleve said.

"What?"

"I told you I know your story. I figured it out, and it fits. Your father owns a lot of corporations, so he's rich. Your mother died when you were born, and you were the only child. You just made up that story about a brother. But as heiress to all of your father's riches, you were a target. You were in danger."

Becky shivered, watching Cleve's face. Does he

know? she wondered. Is this some kind of trick? He's got a lot of details wrong, but he's telling me Devon's story.

"Everyone wants your father's money and his power," Cleve went on. "Naturally you're the weak spot in his defenses. People are always threatening the children of rich people, and if someone kidnapped you, your father would do anything to get you back."

He can't know! Becky thought. Mrs. Nelson said they didn't call the police or anything. They decided Devon would be safest if they just disappeared. She remembered Mrs. Nelson explaining why all of Devon's things were new.

"The call came while we were visiting my husband's parents," Mrs. Nelson had told her." 'You can't keep a child safe every minute.' That's what the man on the phone said. 'You can't watch him every second, and keep him locked up like a prisoner. One of these days you'll be just a little bit careless, and then we'll have him and you won't.' He said other things, too, and then said we should wait for instructions. If we paid enough money, he'd leave our baby alone. He called him by name. Devon. It scared us to death!"

Becky looked at Cleve, realizing how little she knew about him.

"So your father bought this island to hide you on," Cleve was saying. "And he hired that woman to protect you. You're supposed to stay hidden, and that's why you never come to town. No one is even supposed to know you're there." Cleve grinned at her from behind his ice cream. "But I saw you."

"You saw me all right," Becky agreed. He doesn't know anything, she thought. He's just making up a story. He didn't mention a baby. He isn't waiting for me to slip up and say something. "The only problem," she said seriously, "is I have to figure out if you're a good guy or a bad guy. You could have been hired by the people I'm hiding from. Actually, since I'm hiding from everyone, that includes you."

She looked away from him, thinking, then looked back. His eyes looked shadowy, and his face was almost grim.

"Oh, I'm one of the good guys," he said.

Are you? Becky thought. I'm so desperate for company that I'm vulnerable. I'm not sure I can trust my judgment about whether you're dangerous or not.

But then he smiled, and she couldn't help smiling back.

I think Mrs. Nelson's jumpiness is getting to me, she decided. Cleve may be a little eccentric, but he's just a local teenager. He's not involved in the plot against Devon. How could he be? I don't need to be so suspicious.

Really, I don't.

Chapter 5

There is such a thing as nicely weird, Becky thought, trudging up the hill from Cleve's driveway. One arm cradled a half-dozen books; in the other hand she held her flashlight, playing it back and forth across the road.

Or weirdly nice. And I'm sure he didn't know anything. I'm sure he's just a little strange, but nice. I had fun tonight.

She'd sent him firmly to his house, refusing to let him accompany her to Mrs. Nelson's cabin.

"I'll turn my light off," he'd promised. "Your keeper will never know there were two of us."

"Nope," Becky insisted. "If you want me to get out again, you have to go home, and let me go home, too. Alone. Thanks for the ice cream."

She tried the knob at Mrs. Nelson's cabin, grinning as she remembered Cleve's face, pouting in the light of her flash. The evening had gone better than she'd expected, and, except for a few times when she'd caught Cleve giving her strange, thoughtful looks, she'd enjoyed his company.

The cabin door was unlocked, and Becky was glad she didn't have to fumble for a key while juggling an armload of books and her light.

Mrs. Nelson had fallen asleep waiting for her, even though it was barely ten o'clock. Becky had decided to make it an early night in the hopes that her employer would give her more time off if she came home early. She had a moment to study her boss's face, stripped of its usual defenses. She looked younger with the tension gone, and kinder.

Mrs. Nelson woke up when Becky locked the door.

"There's a good library in town," Becky said, setting the books on a chair while she took off her jacket and got a hanger. "It looks so small from the outside. I was afraid they wouldn't have much to choose from. But they did. And they even honored my card from home."

"You have a library card?" Mrs. Nelson sat up, looking horrified. "I didn't think . . . you didn't mention going to the library."

Becky frowned, puzzled by Mrs. Nelson's reaction. "I like to read," she said. "And I have lots of spare time. I needed something to do. Is there a problem? I don't understand."

"Oh, nothing," Mrs. Nelson said. "Never mind. Only . . . could I borrow your card? I like to read, too. I don't have a card."

They'd probably give you one if you asked, Becky

thought. But she said, "Sure," and handed it over. After that, she couldn't bring herself to mention Cleve.

It's not exactly her business, Becky thought. She's not my mother; she's my boss. And what I do on my own time is my own business. I was very careful about what I said. I didn't even scream when I opened my purse to get my library card and found Cheerios in it. I was so calm I don't think Cleve even noticed there was something wrong.

She shook her head. Devon was always dropping things in her purse. He was fascinated with purses, and, of course, his mother never let him touch hers.

But she still felt guilty not mentioning Cleve to Mrs. Nelson. It didn't feel right to be keeping secrets.

Chapter 6

Mrs. Nelson had her usual breakfast of toast and fruit and left early, before Devon was up — also as usual.

Becky ate, did the few dishes, and mopped the kitchen floor. Devon slept late and when he woke up, Becky gave him fruit and cereal and a spoon. He chuckled, banging the tray with the spoon and his fist, happily smearing himself with food. When he finished, Becky gave him a warm cloth and he chewed on it, playing, but also doing a fair job of washing his face and hands.

Becky felt a tiny stab of guilt, knowing she was deliberately ignoring Mrs. Nelson's feeding instructions. Oh, well, she thought. I don't follow the schedule anymore, either. And Devon is a lot happier since I gave it up!

She got out the vacuum and gave Devon his long-handled musical push toy. Together they walked back and forth across the living room floor.

Are we working? Becky wondered. Or playing?

My toy makes more noise, but somehow his seems like more fun.

She glanced out the living room window. There was a spot downhill where the road wound out of the trees and was visible for about forty feet, and as the days went by Becky found herself watching more and more often, hoping for a car, hoping for company that never arrived.

But this time when she looked, she saw Mrs. Nelson's car returning after only two hours. That's strange, Becky thought. She always stays gone all day.

In a few minutes she heard a car door slam, and then Mrs. Nelson opened the front door to the cabin.

"Hello," Becky told her boss. "Home at nine o'clock?"

" 'Lo, Papee," Devon echoed. "Home?"

Papee? Becky thought. That's what I call my grandfather.

Mrs. Nelson dropped the inevitable package on the steps, gave her son a quick kiss, and told Becky, "The washer and dryer are here. On the dock. They'll be bringing them up shortly. We'll have to do something about the baby. And all this stuff. We'll have to hide everything." She fumbled with the playpen, trying to fold it up.

Becky folded the high chair and put it in the huge coat closet, then helped with the playpen. She and Mrs. Nelson hastily gathered blankets, baby dishes, toys, and equipment, stuffing everything in the closet, hurrying, driven by the fear of discovery.

Becky felt as if she were nine years old, scurrying around looking for a hiding place that everybody hadn't already used a dozen times before.

It never worked, she thought. I always got found first. I never was any good at hide-and-seek.

She grabbed two sweatshirts from the closet, one very small sized, and tossed the musical push toy inside.

"Stay close," Mrs. Nelson said nervously. "Only . . . out of sight."

"Right." Becky parked the vacuum in the closet, too, and packed a quick snack. She filled a bottle with apple juice, then watched out the window. When she saw the truck on the road below them, she grabbed the diaper bag, the sweatshirts, and the baby, and slipped out the back door.

"Don't let anyone see him!" Mrs. Nelson said, her face mirroring the fear in her voice.

"I won't," Becky promised. "We're going for a walk," she told Devon, picking him up.

He nodded solemnly, his eyes huge as he craned his neck upward, looking at the tops of the firs.

The stand of trees where Cleve had stood to watch her that day offered the best and nearest cover. But it was also in the direction of his house.

I'm sure it would be safe, she thought. I'm sure Cleve has better things to do than watch for me to step outside the cabin. I can't see that it would matter if he saw Devon, anyway.

Still, she set off in the other direction, carrying the baby, ducking into the woods uphill. Since there were fewer trees, offering less concealment, she decided to go farther into them.

As soon as she figured they were far enough away, she set Devon down to walk, holding his hand. She grinned, thinking of the washer and dryer. Doing laundry in the sink is pretty grim, she thought. I'll be glad to give it up.

She wanted to hike to the lookout point Cleve had told her about, where she could see Canada, the Strait of Juan de Fuca, whales if they happened to be passing, and below her to the right, South End. But it didn't seem like a good place for a baby, especially not one that was supposed to be invisible.

Besides, she thought, I forgot to ask the way. And I don't have any bread crumbs to mark the path in case we get lost. I could leave graham cracker crumbs, I suppose. It just seems a shame that I'm finally out of the house and I can't go anywhere!

When they found a quiet clearing, Becky sat on the soft ground with Devon next to her. She amused him by drawing in the dirt with twigs. She amused herself wondering if Mrs. Nelson's precautions were really necessary.

They live in San Francisco, she thought. There are hundreds of thousands of people in San Francisco. How many of them know Mrs. Nelson or Devon by sight? So what are the chances, even if someone from San Francisco is here, that it would be someone who would know them?

And for there to be any danger, that person

would have to mention Devon to the same person who threatened to kidnap him. Or to someone who knows that person. And no one knows who that is! The chances are so small, it's ridiculous!

I don't think there's any danger at all, she decided. Still I suppose his mother would be a fool to take chances with him. I guess if someone threatened to hurt my baby, I'd run as far and as fast as I could, too.

It's too bad Mr. Nelson has to travel so much. Maybe she'd feel safer if he were around. Maybe she wouldn't look so tense all the time. I wonder if Devon misses his daddy.

Devon had lost interest in Becky's twig drawings and was scooping up dirt with his fists and pouring it on his sweatpants. He laughed and flailed at the dirt, kicking up clouds of dust.

Becky grinned. "Your mommy won't like it," she told Devon. "But you're having a ball. I'd love to let you play in a mud puddle some time. I'll bet you've never even seen mud. What kind of life is that for a baby? Poor kid."

After awhile she picked up Devon and the diaper bag and circled through the thin ranks of trees to where she could see the driveway, and the truck that was still parked there.

"Not yet," she whispered. She started retracing her steps back to the clearing, but Devon said, "Ba-ba?" hopefully.

Oh, Becky thought, glancing at her watch. It is snack time, isn't it? "How about a cracker first?"

she asked. "You can have your bottle later. Oh, brother. Look at your hands! I bring finger food, and your fingers are filthy!"

She cut abruptly back and to her left, toward the stream. The bank was steep, but a little zigzagging path had been worn down to the water and she followed it, carefully balancing Devon on her hip. She pushed up his sleeves, letting him lean over the stream while she held him by the waist. He splashed in the shallow water, cleaning his hands while he played.

The sudden sound of someone whistling carried through the air, over the quiet gurgle of the water, and Becky jumped in surprise and fear, instinctively holding Devon tighter.

The noise came from the direction of the little clearing where Devon had been playing a few minutes before.

Did we leave any tracks? Becky wondered. Any sign that a baby had been there?

The whistled song came closer. It was a lilting, cheery song that Becky found familiar. Maybe "Gypsy Rover," she thought, pulling Devon back and ducking down automatically.

"Da-da?" Devon said, his face lighting up, looking expectant.

"Shh!" Becky whispered.

"Da-da!" Devon called eagerly, wiggling, straining toward the sound.

"Shh!" Becky hissed, pressing his face to her chest to smother his voice. No one's supposed to see you, she thought, feeling a sudden panic. Or hear you! Why did we have to get caught here? Why did someone have to be walking here? Why now?

She scuttled closer to the bank, hoping the steep sides would conceal them, help smother Devon's noises.

You dummy! she told herself, fumbling in the diaper bag for the bottle.

The whistling drew nearer, and Devon twisted his face free. Becky's hand closed around the bottle and she stuck it quickly in Devon's mouth. He sucked thirstily even as he wiggled, looking hopefully up the bank toward the whistling.

It stopped.

The sound stopped, and Becky's heart almost stopped, too. She was afraid to follow Devon's gaze to see who had discovered them. Reluctantly, slowly, she glanced upward.

Chapter 7

No one stood at the top of the bank, looking down at them.

Becky's heart pounded in relief, and she felt a surge of sympathy for Mrs. Nelson. I hadn't realized how scared she must feel, she thought. It must be like this for her all the time.

She cradled Devon to her. I was scared half to death, she thought. And he's not even my baby.

We'll just stay right here for awhile, she decided. I finally found a halfway decent hiding place and I'm not leaving!

The baby's weight was awkward, cutting off the circulation below her knees, and after awhile Becky's legs ached and her calves cramped in protest. Slowly, quietly, she shifted positions, stretching her legs out one at a time. It helped.

The whistling started up again, fainter, and a different song, but still too near for comfort. Becky glanced anxiously at Devon. His bottle was nearly gone. When he finished he would throw it down like he'd thrown his spoon the other night. He would look disgusted that the bottle was empty, and then he would jabber excitedly to prove he wasn't sleepy.

He definitely isn't sleepy now, Becky thought. His eyes smiled brightly at her from behind the bottle.

She eyed the stream and the steep bank. If she remembered right from her evening exploration the day she'd arrived, the stream was shallow all along here, then got deep, swift, and winding beyond the cabin as it headed downhill.

Becky clutched Devon to her and stood cautiously, straightening only to a crouch. Even with the bottle in his mouth, Devon chuckled, evidently enjoying the new game.

Still huddled over, Becky crept into the stream, knowing if she was going to escape she had to do it now, before Devon finished his juice and started making noise. She winced as the cold water seeped into her shoes and soaked her socks. She was grateful the streambed was lined with small stones instead of boulders that she would have to slip and splash around.

She shuffled along with the water, not lifting her feet, not splashing, making very little noise and praying it was little enough.

She was ready when Devon yanked his bottle from his mouth, and caught it before it hit the water. She shifted him quickly to her hip and dropped the bottle into the diaper bag, grabbing the baggie of graham crackers. She handed him two crackers —

one for each hand — and he ate in relative silence.

The banks gradually grew less steep, and Becky judged they'd gone far enough downstream. She scrambled out of the water, glanced hastily around, and took off at a trot toward the cabin.

Devon laughed at the bouncing ride, but Becky was too nervous to enjoy his appreciation.

Her feet were squishing as she ran. Her hands felt clammy, and her heart thudded uncomfortably even though she was sure they were out of danger. My brain knows we're okay, but my body hasn't gotten the message, she thought. The adrenaline has been released and it's still going nuts inside me.

She checked quickly, relieved to see the truck gone from the driveway. She ducked into the house, startling Mrs. Nelson.

"There was someone out walking," she gasped, thrusting Devon into his mother's arms. "We hid, and I'm sure he didn't see us, but I want to go back and see who it was. Did Devon's daddy whistle 'Gypsy Rover'?"

She didn't wait for an answer, but whirled and ran outside again, her mind belatedly registering Mrs. Nelson's awkward grip on her son, and the hurt look on her face as Devon reached out to Becky, calling her. "Bee-Bee?"

Becky's shoes still squished, and she sighed as she ran. I never do anything right, she thought. Now he's going to cry, and she'll be all sickly polite when I get back.

When she reached the stream she slowed her

pace, jogging instead of running, glad to be alongside the stream instead of in it, and hoping that whoever had been whistling would think she was just out for exercise . . . if the person was still there, and if she saw him at all.

She slowed even more as she neared the clearing. Someone was sitting in the shadows cast by the huge firs. It was Cleve, the sun glinting off something in his hands.

Chapter 8

He wasn't whistling; he was sitting about twenty yards from where she'd let Devon wash his hands, sitting beneath one of the firs that lined the stream, holding a knife.

He looked up, surprised. "Well, hi," he said.

Becky stopped jogging. Her first thought was that he seemed genuinely surprised to see her. But her second thought, coming rapidly after the first, was that he looked a little too innocent. And he had a knife! He was slicing at a tree branch that he held in his hands, moving the knife slowly, deliberately. She remembered when he'd asked her if she'd ever cut her hair, how the question had reminded her of knives and crazy people.

He's spying on me, she thought, watching the blade. He was spying the first day I met him, spying when I went to town last night . . . and spying now.

"I sure run into you a lot," she said.

"I sure am glad," Cleve said, grinning.

His smile seemed open and friendly, and he seemed truly glad, but still Becky's suspicions were slow to fade. How well do I know him, anyway? she thought.

"Have a sit," Cleve invited.

Becky sat, trying not to be too obvious as she studied him. She couldn't think of a question that would get him to explain what he was doing here without seeming to accuse him. What do you say to a person who's holding a knife?

This isn't actually our property, she thought. And according to him, this is the way to the lookout point. I guess that makes it a public path or something.

"What does your aunt do?" Cleve asked, the blade glinting again as he slid it down the length of the branch. "For a living, I mean. I see her shopping in town a lot. She seems to enjoy South End. I thought at first she was just vacationing, but she's on the phone a lot at the marina. Most tourists don't know many people on the island, so if they're on the phone a lot during the day, they're calling the office back home. So she's working?"

I thought islanders didn't pry, Becky thought, fascinated with the path of the knife. Cleve looked as if he expected an answer, and Becky finally said, "Oh, she's an executive type. I've never figured out exactly what she does. Buys computer software or something. I guess executives are never really on vacation."

She looked from the knife to Cleve's face to see if he accepted her glib answer.

"She's probably got her own money, then," Cleve said. "Her own credit rating."

There he goes again with the strange questions, she thought, staring at him. It's none of his business, but he looks so grim. "If you mean independent of her husband, I don't know," Becky said stiffly. "I don't talk about that kind of thing with her."

"I guess it's not typical conversation," Cleve agreed, hacking away at the branch. "How old are you?"

Is he grilling me? Becky wondered, getting irritated. She tried to relax. I want to know how old he is, too, she thought. He's just asking friendly questions. He's just being friendly. That's all there is to it.

"Seventeen," she said. "And you?"

"Eighteen," Cleve told her. "A recent graduate of our country's fine public education system." He looked up from the busy knife and grinned. "And I haven't the faintest idea what I'm doing this fall. Or for the rest of my life. It's funny. All I could think about was getting out of high school. Now that I'm out, I have to figure out something to get *in* to."

"College, job, the service, vocational school." Becky ticked the options off on her fingers. "What did I miss? There must be something else you could do." She wished he would put the knife away. She was sure he was only whittling innocently, but it was difficult to concentrate with the glinting threat between them.

"Nothing," Cleve said. "I can always do nothing. I guess that's what I'm doing this summer. But I don't think nothing appeals to me. I'm kind of the loner type — you get that way around here — but I'm already tired of making little sticks out of big sticks. Maybe I ought to get my camera back out and dust it off. I used to take a pretty decent scenery shot."

He snapped his knife shut and tucked it in the rear pocket of his jeans.

Becky sighed in relief.

"Seventeen?" he said. "That's a good age. I was in Denver when I was seventeen. I went to school there. It was either that or commute to Friday Harbor every day. There's an elementary school here, but nothing above that."

"Why Denver?"

"One of my uncles lives there. He shared custody with my other uncle, here. So I'd spend the school year in Denver and the summer on the island."

He lives with his uncles! I'll bet that's why he was so curious about my 'aunt,' Becky thought. He probably wondered if I had a similar arrangement with her. He's not really prying in a spying kind of way, then.

Cleve gave her a piercing, questioning look. "Do

you realize you can't sign a contract at age seventeen?" he asked.

He's getting weird again, Becky thought. "So?" she asked.

"So why would someone sign a contract if they were seventeen, knowing it wasn't legal?"

Becky shrugged. "I don't know. It's an interesting question. Why does anyone do anything if it's not legal? Maybe they do it *because* it's illegal. Maybe they don't know it's illegal. Maybe they don't care. Why do you care? Why did you ask me that question?"

"Oh, I don't know," Cleve said casually. "Do you like the cabin?"

"It's fine," she said. "I've got to go. I've been gone too long." She headed back, walking fast, angry, wondering why he had been grilling her.

I'm the one who has a reason to be suspicious of him, she thought. Why is he acting like he's suspicious of me? What is wrong with him, anyway?

Chapter 9

Mrs. Nelson met Becky at the cabin as if she'd been watching for her. She handed her a spoon that was covered with unappetizing-looking bits of something green.

"I don't think he likes peas," Mrs. Nelson said, looking grim.

Becky could hear Devon fussing in the kitchen.

"Did you see who it was?" Mrs. Nelson asked.

"What?" Becky asked. "Oh. In the woods, you mean?" She hesitated. If I tell her I didn't find anyone, I'll frighten her, Becky thought. She'll be wondering who was there and imagine the worst. Besides, I did find someone. It's one thing to not mention meeting him on the way to town, but this is different.

Still, she didn't want to mention his name, or discuss him with her boss. "It was just a neighbor," she said. "He said he lives in the next cabin down the hill. He was just out for a walk in the woods, I guess. There's a lookout point if you follow the stream uphill, so I guess anyone who wants to look at the whales from there would be on the same path."

Devon started crying.

"You'd better feed him," Mrs. Nelson said, looking strained. "He needs to eat all his peas. I won't have him growing up to be a picky eater. I'm going back to town."

Becky was glad to escape to the kitchen . . . to avert further questions. Devon smiled when he saw her, reaching for her. He cried, "Owie!" pointing to his leg.

He'd managed to get his leg twisted beneath him, and Mrs. Nelson had the safety strap tightened too much to give him room to squirm and free himself.

Becky loosened the strap, straightened Devon's leg, and gave him a hug. Outside, she heard the door thunk shut on Mrs. Nelson's car, heard the engine fire smoothly.

"First off, we lose the peas," Becky told Devon, rinsing them down the sink. "Second, even though I'm ruining your Mom's plans for you, we let you do the work." She got a clean spoon for Devon, and he laughed, banging with enthusiasm while Becky warmed sweet potatoes, which he loved, to replace the peas, which he did not.

While he was feeding himself, along with the tray, his face, his bib, his hair, and the floor, Becky thought back to the near-encounter in the woods.

Devon said Da-da, she thought. When Cleve whistled . . . do we know it was Cleve whistling? I

41

guess not for sure, but it's a fair assumption. Anyway, I wonder. . . .

She whistled "Gypsy Rover," softly, watching Devon's face. He looked up eagerly, but his excitement faded to a puzzled expression when he realized the song was coming from Becky.

Hmm, she thought. A definite reaction. "I'll bet you miss your daddy," she said.

"Da?"

"Yeah, Da," Becky agreed. "I wonder if your mother has any pictures of him she could show you. She could let you talk on the phone, too. She says she calls him all the time."

But she hasn't thought of it herself, Becky thought grimly. If I suggest it, that's criticism. She doesn't like criticism. She sighed and started the laundry, her mood improving with each load. It was such a pleasure to have machines to do the work!

That evening Becky watched Mrs. Nelson and Devon during their scheduled fifteen minutes together before bedtime. Mrs. Nelson sat on the couch with Devon beside her. She showed him her day's purchases, but didn't let him touch them. He squirmed and fussed, then tried to get down to play, but his mother hauled him back up and told him to sit still and behave.

Becky sighed. It was a familiar scene. Mrs. Nelson just doesn't understand babies, she thought. A one-year-old can't sit and admire a new silk blouse and a purse. If he can't play with it or eat it, why should he be interested?

The scheduled fifteen minutes had originally been written down as a half hour, but after two nights, Mrs. Nelson had decided he was too fussy to enjoy that long a visit. The mother-son interaction time had been shortened, and bedtime had been moved up.

Becky glanced at the clock. Time was slipping by. When Devon went to bed, Mrs. Nelson would go back to town, or to her room to make calls. If Becky didn't say anything soon, it would be too late for today. Tomorrow she might have lost her nerve.

She took a deep breath. "I remember when my parents went on business trips when I was little," Becky said. "I always missed them so much. But I had pictures to look at, and they called every day. Talking on the phone helped. I felt better. Devon's lucky you don't have to travel, too. Then he'd be missing both of you instead of just his father."

She was afraid to look at Mrs. Nelson to see her expression, but the silence was expressive enough.

Becky flipped a page in her book, pretending to read, hoping she seemed nonchalant, and hoping it had NOT sounded like a suggestion or a criticism.

"I do not believe a child of this age is capable of understanding the passage of time," Mrs. Nelson finally said.

Becky winced at the frost in her voice.

"As far as Devon understands, it's just like his father has gone to work, as he does every morning. An hour or a day or a month are all the same to a child. Do you have any special reason for implying that Devon misses his father?"

Aside from his reaction to the whistling, which I asked about and you chose not to mention? Becky thought.

Mrs. Nelson's voice, as she asked the question, had gone from frosty to superior to fake-casual, and Becky wondered why her boss had been so careful to make her question sound unimportant.

I'm missing something here, Becky thought. She sat up straighter, then realized how suspicious that looked. She slumped again, trying to look as if she hadn't noticed a thing. "No," she said. "I was just thinking about being little. It seems so easy to have everyone taking care of you. Then I remembered my parents being gone so much and I guess I was being sympathetic. It can't be as easy as it looks to be a baby."

"You do have a flair for the dramatic," Mrs. Nelson said.

She sounds relieved, Becky thought. Or is she pretending not to notice my reaction, like I pretended not to notice hers? Am I nuts, or is something funny going on here?

"If you're not going to be busy tonight, I'd like to go back into town," Becky said. "I haven't had a chance to do any sightseeing or shopping yet."

"Oh." Mrs. Nelson handed Devon to Becky, looking suddenly rushed. "I forgot. I have a meeting I need to attend. Sorry."

As she rushed around gathering her purse, checking for car keys, finding her coat, Becky soothed Devon and thought, I don't think I'm nuts. And I do think there is something weird going on. Definitely.

Chapter 10

Becky sighed, staring out Devon's window. The night was so deep she felt disoriented, as if she were staring into absolute nothingness, into a black hole in space. The forest outside the cabin waited, dark and empty . . . or was it? Tonight it seemed full of noises and possibilities, full of everything but hope.

"Never," she muttered. "I will never get into town again. There can't be that many emergency meetings and forgotten appointments." She thumped her fist against the soft mattress on Devon's changing table. "She doesn't want me to leave. There's something out there, and she thinks I'll find it . . . or it'll find me."

Behind her Devon caught his breath in a sigh and turned over. She could hear him suck briefly at his fingers, then stop. His breathing deepened again.

Every night that she seems to be staying home, I ask if I can go, and she suddenly remembers she has to leave. Every time. If I don't mention going out, she stays home. That can't be coincidence. Not that many times. Not after two weeks.

I've been here a month and I've been to town exactly once.

Once.

I'm a prisoner here.

Chapter 11

In the morning she shook her head at herself.

Prisoner indeed! she thought, making her bed.

The birds were singing outside, the sun was warm through the window, and last night's black hole seemed to belong in a science-fiction novel.

Becky sang as she made herself breakfast. "Good morning," she said cheerfully to Mrs. Nelson. "We can't seem to coordinate our schedules, so why don't you just let me know when you can spare me, and I'll go to town then. If I go home at the end of the summer without something exotic from here, I'll never be able to show my face in school. I need at least three trips to town."

"Three?" Mrs. Nelson seemed uncertain how to take Becky's cheerful mood.

"Three," Becky said firmly. "I have to scout out the shops. I have to find presents for my family, including three hard-to-impress younger brothers. I have to find presents for my friends, and some things for myself. That'll take at least three trips."

"Well," Mrs. Nelson said faintly, heading out the door. "I'm pretty busy the next week or so, but I'll let you know."

The next week or so! Becky thought, her spirits fading. I can't take another week without going cabin-crazy.

She helped Devon wave out the window. "Say bye-bye to Mama," she told him.

"Ma-ma?" he said hopefully.

Becky pointed out the window.

"Bye-bye, Pa-pee," he called. "Bye-bye."

They watched for the car down the hill, waving, and as Becky turned away from the window, the phone rang. They both jumped.

I don't think I've ever heard it ring, Becky thought.

" 'Lo?" Devon said, and Becky laughed.

The phone was in Mrs. Nelson's bedroom, behind a closed and locked door. Still it rang shrilly, sounding loud and demanding.

"Every cell in my body is programmed to answer that," Becky told Devon. "But it's your mom's business phone. No personal calls allowed. I'm not even supposed to touch the phone. Neither are you. We're stuck, listening. Ignoring it if we can."

It rang on and on until Becky's resolve began to dissolve. What if it's Cleve? she thought. Or Mom and Dad? If there was a problem, they might call information and get the number.

She gave Devon his food and cleaned the kitchen while he ate, her nerves ringing with the phone.

Finally it quit, and Becky listened gratefully to the hum of the fridge and the vroom-vroom noise Devon made playing with his truck on his high-chair tray, and thought the quiet noises were the most pleasant sounds she'd ever heard.

Half an hour later the phone started ringing again. Becky vacuumed through the rings, wishing she could unplug the phone. I would, if it weren't in her bedroom, she thought. If the door weren't locked.

Half an hour after that it rang again, for a full five minutes as Becky timed it. Then an hour passed before it rang again.

I will go totally nuts if this keeps up, Becky thought. I have nothing except the vacuum cleaner to drown it out with — no TV, no radio, no tape player. Why didn't I bring my tape player and some tapes?

The phone made Devon cranky, too. It echoed through the small cabin like a nagging conscience, inescapable and shrill. The baby had gotten up early, so Becky put him down for an early nap.

The phone woke him after about forty-five minutes, even though the noise was fainter in his room than anywhere else in the house.

We must be conditioned to the noise, Becky thought, trying to soothe him back to sleep. But instead of getting used to it, it bothers us more and more.

Devon wouldn't go back to sleep, so Becky gave

up on his nap. The phone only rang twice more, but by the time Mrs. Nelson came home, both Becky and Devon were cranky, tired, and in bad moods.

"That darned phone!" Becky snapped, slapping dinner on the table in the pans she'd cooked it in. "It never stopped ringing! It drove me nuts!"

Her boss's look of horror would normally have stopped Becky mid-tirade, but she didn't even pause. "I'm ready to scream! I never want to hear another telephone ring as long as I live!"

"You didn't answer it, did you?" Mrs. Nelson sagged against the table.

"No, I didn't!" Becky was almost shouting. "Maybe I should have. Then it would have quit ringing. Do you have any idea how crazy a phone can make you? It's like torture, ringing and ringing and ringing."

Mrs. Nelson grabbed the edge of the table.

Becky quit ranting and stared. "Are you okay?" she asked.

"Just a dizzy spell," Mrs. Nelson said.

Really? Becky wondered.

"I skipped lunch. I'm sure I'll be fine once I eat."

Becky helped her into a chair and quickly heaped a plate with taco salad. "Eat," she urged. "I thought you were going to faint. You scared me."

What happened? she wondered, watching her employer eat. Was it a fainting spell because she missed lunch? Or was it because the phone rang? Why would that frighten her? What is going on?

She glanced at Devon and then back at Mrs. Nelson, frowning, wondering.

Mrs. Nelson returned her gaze, her own face unreadable. "After Devon's asleep, you can go into town," she said.

Chapter 12

Devon went to bed early after his disrupted nap, and it was barely seven o'clock when Becky set off, her flashlight in her purse for the walk home.

The sun was low but still warm, and Becky slowed her steps, enjoying the feeling of freedom, relishing the fact that she was walking away from the cabin, by herself.

No responsibilities, she thought. No boss. No little boy to claim any of my attention. No noise. No ringing phone.

I'm out! Free! I have a night off!

Her face lit up in a smile, and her steps quickened until she deliberately slowed again, stretching the feeling of freedom.

And giving Cleve a chance to notice and join me, she thought honestly. I think I want to see him. I guess seeing him is better than not seeing anyone!

But she passed the drive to his place, and he didn't join her. She was disappointed, but too excited at having a free evening to let her spirits fall for long.

The evening was peaceful, the feeling of aloneness was refreshing, and Becky was grateful until nagging questions arose in her mind and suspicions began to set in.

She gave me the night off because I started wondering why she panicked, Becky realized. She read my reaction just like I read hers. She knew a night off was the one thing that would make me forget her, and why the phone ringing made her almost faint.

So why *did* it make her almost faint? She uses the phone for business all the time. Her husband and her coworkers must have the number, even though no one ever calls. She didn't say anything about it being someone from the office, though. She didn't say she'd have to try to find out who was calling. She only asked if I'd answered the phone, and acted faint.

Becky wondered for awhile, but didn't come to any conclusions, and thinking about her evening in town was more exciting.

Shopping! she thought. The library . . . oh, I forgot to ask for my card back. Well, I'll skip the library this time, then. After I go shopping I'll stop at a coffee shop, and then I'll go to the boatyard and ask for Cleve. I'll bet someone there could help me find him.

But she found herself at the boatyard first. It was a confusion of wooden docks, colorful sails, and wandering, shouting people. Becky stood at the edge of the water, looking around.

Eventually she sorted through the noise and motion enough to realize there were gas pumps on the left docks, and people working the pumps. Employees.

The first man she asked frowned thoughtfully. "He was here earlier. Jake!" he roared.

An old man stuck his head out of what had to be an office, though it looked like a changing room at the beach.

"You seen Cleve?"

"Yup." Jake pulled his head back in the office.

"Where is he?" the man yelled.

Jake turned back around, looking irritated. "Don't know."

"Where was he when you saw him?"

"Over there." He stepped out and pointed. "Loading Calvin on the air-evac. Silly fool went and broke his ankle. Fifty years climbing this island and still takes a nosedive down Babyface." Jake clumped into his office.

"Sheriff fell off a cliff," the man translated. "I forgot Cleve was there. Helped load him. That was some excitement, I tell you. We get tourists falling off Babyface. Lean over too far looking at the views. But locals!" He paused, snorting.

Becky decided he was laughing.

"Could happen to anyone, I guess. Anyway, easiest thing for you to do is go sit at Josephina's. You can see everything from there and have a good cup of coffee while you're at it. You might see him. And if he shows up here first, I'll send him there."

He obligingly pointed out Josephina's, a watershed-turned-coffee shop that loomed over the town, perched on a blufflike hillside, bright umbrellas dotting the lawn.

Becky stopped at a few shops along the way, finding T-shirts for her brothers and a pair of graceful whale earrings for her mother, then climbed the winding wooden sidewalk to Josephina's.

As the evening darkened, the town brightened, with the boatyard and the marina lighting up the coast, and the lights of the other islands beckoning from a distance.

Becky ordered an iced tea and relaxed at an outdoor table, watching the coastline, listening to the far-off, lonely wail of the ferries as they pulled into or out of port.

After awhile she saw Cleve making his way across the lawn toward her. He waved, then joined her, looking worried.

"I can't believe it," he said, without saying hello first. "Calvin's lived here forever. How could he fall off Babyface?"

"What *is* Babyface?" Becky demanded.

"Oh." Cleve looked distracted. "It's the whale-watching point I told you about. There's a cliff — a pretty easy climb, unless it's wet. It ends in a series of ledges . . . perfect landing spots, no matter what the tide is. Its real name is Boniface, but it's where we take the beginning rock climbers to learn the basic skills, so we all call it Babyface."

"Were you there?" Becky asked. "I thought the man at the boatyard said you were with the sheriff."

"The whales were out." Cleve looked excited, briefly, before he frowned again. "I was setting up my tripod. I told you about that, right?"

"You mentioned your camera," Becky said.

"Right. Calvin used to take a lot of pictures with me. He taught me how, in fact. When I was little. Anyway, I was setting up my tripod, so I had my back turned. I heard him yell and when I ran over, he was already down on the ledge."

Cleve shook his head, remembering. "It doesn't look that far down until you see someone you know crumpled up at the bottom. I was never so glad in my life as when Calvin started yelling at me to come around in my boat. He could have broken his neck. In fact, I don't know why he didn't."

"The guy at the boatyard said something about air-evac."

"Helicopter," Cleve said glumly. "We've got a good clinic here, and they did the X ray. But they said the ankle was shattered. He had to go to a real hospital to get it fixed."

Cleve looked so worried that Becky couldn't help feeling sorry for the Calvin she'd never met. She put her hand on Cleve's arm. "He'll be okay," she said. "Doctors are used to fixing ankles."

Cleve tried to smile. "You're right," he said. "I

know you are. But I can't help feeling responsible. I was there. And I've known Calvin forever. We go back a long way."

"He'll be fine," Becky repeated. "And the other sheriffs can take over till he's better."

Cleve made a face. "There are no other sheriffs," he said. "Calvin's been the only law-enforcement officer on Sebastian for twenty years. We'll just have to cross our fingers and hope no tourists start rioting or stealing or breaking things till Calvin is up to the capture."

"Is it always tourists?" Becky asked. "Don't locals ever do anything wrong?"

"Never," Cleve said solemnly. "Who would dare? Everybody knows everybody. The only people with secrets are the tourists. Speaking of tourists . . ." Cleve lowered his voice. "This is where your boss always comes. Mornings and afternoons. She sits over there." He pointed.

Becky looked across to the table Cleve indicated. It was at the far edge of the lawn, overlooking the water.

"I see," she whispered, and as she spoke the words, she did see. She knew now what Mrs. Nelson did in town every day, at least mornings and afternoons.

Chapter 13

She watches the ferry, Becky realized. She's trying to see if anyone lands who might be looking for Devon.

She frowned. But how would she know? If she knows who to watch for, she could have just told the police. She could have told me. She could have hired a private detective to keep track of him and then she'd know ahead of time if he was getting near. But if she doesn't know who to watch for, what good does it do to watch? How would she know if she was seeing anything?

She thought it over, trying to see if she'd missed an angle, but if she had, she couldn't figure out what. If a person is watching, she thought, then they're watching for something or someone and they think they'll recognize it when they see it.

"Do you want to spend your night off sitting here?" Cleve asked. "Seems to me we ought to be doing something exciting. Would you like a guided tour of South End?"

Becky grabbed her windbreaker, and they headed toward the steep and winding path down the hill from Josephina's. They stopped first at the boatyard where Cleve pointed out his own sailboat, a small, neat craft painted white with black trim.

"Next time you come, we'll take a moonlight sail," he promised. "And if there's no wind, I happen to have a motor, too. I installed it myself. It's the best kind of a sailboat — one that doesn't get stalled if there's no wind."

Or maybe we'll do something else, Becky thought.

They wandered through town, Cleve pointing out the historic buildings and the different shops. They did some late shopping, walked along the shore, then stopped at one of the little seaside restaurants that was set almost as far up the hill as Josephina's.

They ordered bowls of chowder and argued good-naturedly about the last piece of crusty bread that had come with it.

"You had three chunks, and I only had two," Cleve said. "Since you had more, I should get the last one."

Becky shook her head. "Wrong. You live here, so you can get more bread any time you want. And besides, I'm the guest and you're the host and the host is always supposed to give in to the guest. That's polite."

Finally, grumbling, Cleve split the bread in two, offering one piece to Becky. His eyes had a mischievous look.

"Put both pieces on the table," Becky demanded. "I get to choose the one I want."

"What? That's not fair!"

"Of course, it is," Becky told him. "One person divides, the other person gets first choice."

"Then what good does it do me to cut myself a big half?" Cleve asked, reluctantly producing the other piece of bread.

Becky pounced on it. "None," she said, biting into it quickly. "That's the whole point. Crime doesn't pay."

Cleve's face sobered suddenly and he gave her another of his odd, almost-evaluating looks.

Becky swallowed hard.

What *is* it with this guy? she thought. She put the rest of her bread back on the table. The fun had gone out of the game.

"You get so bizarre," she said, shaking her head at him. "Out of the middle of nowhere, you suddenly turn strange. Well, thanks for a lot of fun." She reached into her purse and felt around. Her hand touched a wad of bills. Becky didn't care how much money it was. She didn't want to owe Cleve anything.

She grabbed it out of her purse and dropped the wad on the table as she whirled, grabbing her windbreaker. She left quickly, wondering what, if anything, sparked his sudden mood changes. She shivered, remembering how rapidly and completely he had gone from friendly to . . . what? Not unfriendly, she decided. Just distant. Weird.

Becky folded her windbreaker collar up against the chilly breeze that was blowing off the water. He isn't going to ruin my night out, she decided, hurrying down the wooden steps and across the first flat section of sidewalk, pausing before the next set of stairs to let an older couple finish their climb.

The man was heavy and stopped often to catch his breath, his wife waiting patiently. During one of his pauses, Becky heard footsteps clattering down the stairs behind her.

She briefly debated edging by the panting man, but he and his wife had nearly reached the top. Becky sighed. If it's Cleve, I'll just ignore him, she decided.

The hillside was well-lit, especially the sidewalk and stairs, with nothing to hide behind. Becky waited, and the second the couple had passed her, she started for the stairs.

"Could I at least apologize?"

It was Cleve.

She stopped, her decision to ignore him forgotten at the pain in his voice. She turned.

"I'm sorry," Cleve said. "I just have an overactive imagination, I guess. I keep imagining . . . things."

"What do you mean?" Becky asked. She started down the stairs and Cleve joined her, his hands in his pockets, his boots thumping on the wooden steps.

"Calvin," Cleve said.

"You always do that," Becky told him. "You give

one- or two-word answers, as if that explains every-thing. Well it doesn't. You have to say more than just 'Calvin.' "

"Cal and I were the only ones up there," he said slowly. "But Calvin couldn't have fallen. I can't imagine him falling. He's lived here all his life."

"You can't have it both ways," Becky pointed out. "Either he could fall or he couldn't. Not both. And since he did, then I guess he could. Unless . . ." Becky glanced over at Cleve's face. "You can't mean he was pushed."

"I guess I can't," Cleve said. "Since I was the only other person there. But I've gotten some funny looks. I guess everybody else thinks he couldn't have fallen, too."

They reached the bottom of the bluff, and Becky turned towards the shop-lined main street. So that's why you looked at me so oddly, she thought. You thought I was giving you one of those funny looks, too. You thought my comment had a double mean-ing.

"Accidents happen," she said, tugging Cleve's hand out of his pocket and holding it. "All you have to do is wait for word from Calvin. He knows he fell, and once he tells people that, they'll quit giving you funny looks."

"I guess," Cleve agreed. "Maybe I'm just too sensitive. People ask me questions about what hap-pened, and I hear suspicions. When people ask how he could have fallen, what I hear them saying is he couldn't fall, so he must have been pushed . . . which means I must have pushed him. I'm only half-local, you know, since I spend my winters in Denver. That makes my status questionable, I guess. I'm not trusted as much as the real locals."

They walked a little farther, and Cleve said, "It's just a little difficult knowing people are looking at you and wondering if you tried to murder the sheriff."

Chapter 14

At Cleve's driveway Becky tugged on his arm. "This is where you get off," she said.

They'd walked through South End, admiring the window displays, then walked the piers at midnight, heading home, absorbing the quiet, eternal slap of waves, the peace that Becky decided could only come when the stars were bright and the water lapped calmly at the shore, and the rest of the world slept.

She could almost feel the gentle pounding of the waves in Cleve's hand as she held it, could almost feel a link between the sea and her heart pulsing in their hands. And when he kissed her, it was almost a kiss of the waves and the earth and the tiny, rugged island itself.

"It doesn't seem right," Cleve whispered, glancing up the hill. "I'd rather walk you home."

Becky shook her head.

Her flashlight drooped in her hand as he put his

arms around her, then shone on the trees as she hugged him back.

"Oh, here," Cleve said, fumbling in his jacket pocket. He pushed something into her hand. "You dropped this."

Oh, Becky thought, recognizing the wad of money she'd left on the table. "I'm willing to pay my own way," she said.

"Not with this." Cleve's voice was amused. "Besides, it was my treat. I'm the host, remember?"

Becky dropped the wad into her purse.

"See you . . . sometime," Cleve said.

Sometime, Becky thought, trudging up the hill to the cabin.

Sometime . . . when? When will I get out again?

The look on Mrs. Nelson's face was half anger and half relief. "Do you have any idea how late it is?" she demanded.

"I thought it was my night off," Becky said. And since I don't seem to get many of them, I decided to make the best of the one I had, she added silently.

Mrs. Nelson glared, and Becky wondered if she would be fired. It wouldn't matter too much, she decided.

But she knew it would. She was counting on the generous paycheck. It would go a long way toward paying college expenses that her parents couldn't afford.

Besides, Becky realized, except for my boss, I like this job. I love Devon, the island is beautiful, and Cleve is turning out to be not bad at all. Most of the time.

Mrs. Nelson's glare grew angrier.

Devon cried out from his bedroom. "Bee-bee!" he wailed.

"He's been doing that all night!" Mrs. Nelson snapped. "It's driving me nuts! I've been trying to get some work done, but he keeps waking up and calling for you."

Becky ran in to hug Devon, and he held her tightly back, saying her name over and over. She took him from his crib and walked the floor with him, hushing him, singing softly.

She cradled him gratefully, relieved. . . . Mrs. Nelson would never fire her if Devon liked her so much!

But along with the relief she felt trapped. Mrs. Nelson would also never give her another night off if Devon cried the whole time she was gone!

"You silly baby," she chided gently. "Why did you wake up? You always stay asleep. If you'd stayed asleep, you'd never have known I was gone." I wonder, she thought. I'll bet somehow your mother woke you up. Maybe she wanted to hold you while you were sleeping. That might have been enough to wake you.

When he fell asleep at last, she settled him back in his crib and pulled the blanket up. "Good-night," she whispered. She felt sorry that Mrs. Nelson hadn't been able to get him back to sleep. There's something rewarding about soothing a crying baby, she thought, feeling satisfied as she headed for the living room.

"He's asleep," she told Mrs. Nelson. "I wonder why he woke up. He never does that."

"I don't think it's a good idea for you to be gone. It seems to upset him."

Becky felt her shoulders slump. The dreaded words, she thought. No more nights off.

She took a deep breath and before she could chicken out, she said, "I can't stay cooped up here all the time."

"I've been thinking about that, too," Mrs. Nelson said.

"You told me I'd be working while Devon was awake," Becky said. "I knew I'd be in the cabin for twelve hours. But I thought the rest of the time would be mine, to spend how I wanted to. I can't stay in here twenty-four hours a day. If you don't want me gone at night, I'll take time off in the morning or afternoon, whichever you'd prefer, but I can't stay indoors all summer."

"I've ordered a screen," Mrs. Nelson said calmly.

"What?"

"A screen that people can't see through," Mrs. Nelson said. "It folds out to enclose a good-sized area, and will make an outdoor play yard for Devon. He's a quiet child, most of the time. He can play quietly outside, and you can work on your tan. No one will be able to see him, and you won't be cooped up inside the whole time."

Becky felt her advantage slipping away, and she couldn't think how to regain it. "I still need time off," she protested. But her protest didn't have much force to it.

As she got ready for bed, she remembered the wad of money Cleve had returned. I wonder how much I tried to give him, she thought, recalling his amused comment.

The second she felt the wad she knew something was peculiar. I don't remember putting any money in a rubber band, she thought, pulling it out.

Her face burned, and she dropped the napkin-wrapped wad on her bed, not knowing whether to laugh or cry.

I can't believe I did that, she thought, pulling the rubber band off the napkin. Cleve had re-wrapped the parcel carefully, making it look undisturbed.

But he saw what it was, Becky thought. He wouldn't have sounded so amused if he hadn't looked.

She remembered Devon dropping it on the floor at dinner the other night, remembered picking it up and idly folding it in a napkin so he wouldn't see it and want it back. She even remembered wrapping a rubber band around it.

She did not remember putting it in her purse. She knew perfectly well that Devon had put it there.

I can't believe I tried to pay for dinner with a pacifier, she thought, covering her face with her hands. Cleve must think I'm the strangest person he's ever run across.

I'm going to have to do some fast talking to get out of this.

She turned off her light and climbed in bed, the baby's pacifier still lying somewhere on the covers.

How am I going to explain this one? she thought. I have to keep Devon a secret. That's the whole reason I can't go to town — so I can keep Devon a secret.

She sat up in bed. Wait a minute, she thought. Nobody's supposed to see me or Devon. Why is it okay if people see her? If she's worried about the baby being recognized . . . anyone who would recognize the baby would recognize her!

Nobody knows me at all, but somebody knows her. The person who followed her and threatened her baby knows her, and that's the person she's worried about! If she's so frightened for Devon that he has to be invisible and I can't go to town, why can she go? Why would she spend time at the marina, which is the most public place on the island, if someone might recognize her?

If she's so worried about Devon, why isn't she hiding, too?

Chapter 15

Becky counted twenty-five rings before the noise finally stopped.

I can't stand another day of this, she thought. I won't put up with it!

In fifteen minutes the caller tried again.

How can it sound so loud? Becky thought, plugging her ears with her fingers. Mrs. Nelson's door is closed, and it still sounds as if the phone is in here with us.

Devon started whining.

The phone finally stopped, and Becky sighed. She wished they had the screen already so she could take Devon outside and escape the noise.

It was only about ten minutes before the ringing started again. Becky slammed the frying pan into the sink and yelled, "Shut up!" which startled Devon so badly that he ran to her, holding onto her legs and sobbing.

I've got two choices, Becky decided, comforting the baby. I can break into Mrs. Nelson's room and throw the phone out the window, or I can take Devon outside all day.

She remembered Mrs. Nelson's speech her first day on the job. She'd given Becky a tour of the cabin, but only pointed at one closed door. "That's my room," she'd said. "Devon isn't allowed in there at all. I keep that door locked at all times. My room is part office, you understand. Devon could do a frightening amount of damage to my confidential papers. Of course, your cleaning duties don't include that room."

Didn't Bluebeard have a room like that? Becky thought. A room no one was allowed to enter. If I remember right, his new bride got too curious and finally opened the door, finding all of Bluebeard's previous wives — dead — and an empty space ready for her.

She looked at the knob on Mrs. Nelson's door. There was only a little round hole for the key.

Becky grinned suddenly. I can pick that lock with a nail, she thought. Or a screwdriver. Anything long and skinny.

She put Devon in his playpen, found an ice pick in the kitchen, and inserted the thin shaft into the hole in the doorknob. She pushed it straight in, turning the knob at the same time. As easily as if she'd used a key, Mrs. Nelson's door opened.

Becky half-expected a loud creak of protest from the hinges, but the door slid open quietly, revealing an ordinary bedroom. There was a bed, a dresser, a vanity table, and a small desk with a box of stationery and the telephone on it.

She let out the breath she hadn't realized she'd been holding, let it out in a small laugh, and stepped into the room.

An alarm went off.

Becky jumped, immediately feeling like a thief caught in the act, almost as immediately realizing it wasn't an alarm at all. It was the phone ringing again.

She reached behind the phone and disconnected the line.

The silence made Devon laugh.

Becky took a quick, guilty look around Mrs. Nelson's room, noticing the vanity covered with an incredible array of makeup and perfume, and noticing, too, the complete lack of pictures or any other personal items. The room was perfectly neat. Except for the cosmetics, it could have been a hotel room after the cleaning crew had finished.

She's a better housekeeper than I am, Becky thought, closing the door and lifting Devon out of his playpen.

She played with Devon, working during his naps, and kept an eye on the window, watching the road where she could see Mrs. Nelson's car down the hill if she happened to come home early.

Around five o'clock, when it was time to start dinner, Becky left Devon playing on the living room floor and opened Mrs. Nelson's door again.

The phone sat silently on the fake-wood desk, looking too innocent to have caused such an uproar. I didn't look at the desk carefully when I unplugged the phone, Becky thought, rapping on the wood grain. No wonder the ringing is so loud. This is a metal desk with shelf paper on it. It magnifies the ringing. I could have just moved the phone onto the bed so the sound was muffled.

The end of the phone wire was no longer on the desktop.

I guess it slipped down in back, she thought, leaning over, reaching behind. She could feel the phone jack and followed the wire from that end, pulling it up. The wire caught the edge of the box of stationery and flipped it onto the floor.

Becky muttered under her breath, worrying about Mrs. Nelson's return. She was due any minute.

She quickly plugged the phone back in, then knelt and gathered scattered papers and envelopes.

All I need is for her to come in and find me rummaging through her private papers in her carefully locked bedroom, she thought, grabbing, neatening, and stuffing papers in the box. She hardly trusts me as it is . . . what?

Becky looked blankly at the envelope in her hand. It was a phone bill, opened, addressed to a post office box in South End, Sebastian Island, Washington. It was addressed to Rebecca Collier.

I don't understand, Becky thought. That's my name.

Chapter 16

Becky stared for a full minute, her mind blank.

She poked at the papers and envelopes she'd been stuffing into the stationery box. Rent receipt, made out to Rebecca Collier, signed by John Hillyer. Receipt for one washing machine and one clothes dryer, paid in full, delivery accepted by Rebecca Collier. Bank statement, showing a balance of $42,008.42 for the account of Rebecca Collier.

She looked up, her face blank, as Mrs. Nelson walked into the room.

Chapter 17

Mrs. Nelson's face went through three distinct expressions: shock, anger, and dismay.

"You've been using my name," Becky said.

"You've been going through my things," Mrs. Nelson said icily.

Becky shook her head. "It was an accident. The phone was ringing again. I unplugged it. I knocked the box off the desk plugging the phone back in, and saw the papers with my name on them. I had to pick the lock to go into your room, and I know I shouldn't have, but it was either that or quit. I couldn't take one more day of the phone ringing."

Devon had followed his mother into the room, and Becky gathered him up and kissed the top of his head. "What I did was an accident," she said. "What you did was not. The phone, the rent, even the washer and dryer — it's all in my name. I looked at my phone bill. Not one call is to New York. You called everywhere but where you said you were calling. You're lying to me about everything."

Mrs. Nelson's face went blank, her eyes looking up and to the right. Becky could swear it was the same thing her little brothers did when they were planning a quick cover story to keep out of trouble.

"I'm supposed to be protecting Devon," Becky said angrily. "How can I if I don't know what's going on? You've been lying to me from the very first day, and I want to know the truth!" Becky was almost shouting, but Mrs. Nelson only grew pale.

"I think you'd better tell me," Becky ordered.

Mrs. Nelson nodded. "I'm hiding Devon from his father." She wiped at her eyes with her fingertips, and Becky handed her a tissue.

"I was crazy about Franklin," she said. "He had those melting brown eyes and that beautiful smile. He was handsome and he was fun. We had fun together. And he was rich. I suppose if I hadn't been so in love, I'd have objected to his jealousy earlier. I just thought it proved he loved me. I thought it was cute."

She sighed, dabbing her cheeks. "As soon as we were married, it got worse. It was like he owned me. It wasn't cute at all. I couldn't leave the house without the chauffeur, and of course, Franklin chose the chauffeur. Even if I took a walk, the chauffeur followed me in the limo.

"Franklin chose my maid, too. Her main job was to keep track of what I did and who came over."

Mrs. Nelson's laugh was bitter. "And the phone was routed through his office. Every call I made or received had to go through his secretary first, and she recorded them. I thought . . . I really thought having a baby would prove to him that I loved him. I thought he'd ease up."

Becky thought her boss looked pathetic with her pale, tearstreaked face. I thought adults were supposed to be smart, she thought.

"I'm afraid it was a terrible mistake," Mrs. Nelson went on. "It made him worse. I didn't think things could get worse, but I was wrong." Her face was still as she looked inward on remembered scenes, the horror making her blue eyes seem huge and dark.

"He burned all my old letters and pictures," Mrs. Nelson said, shivering. "He burned my prom dress because he said another man's hands had held me while I was wearing it. He made me describe every date I'd ever been on, every kiss, every word of love any man had ever whispered to me. He made me tell him again and again, and it made him furious when I did, but even madder if I tried to refuse.

"He found my yearbooks from school. He read everything people had written in them, and then he accused me of awful things. Then he burned the yearbooks. He burned my whole past. He didn't want me to have anything except him. And Devon. He was so eager for Devon to be born.

"But when he was born, Franklin didn't even want me to have him. Jealousy is bad enough, but he was obsessed."

Mrs. Nelson had started pacing in her room, but she obviously felt too confined in the small space.

She moved into the living room and Becky followed, still holding Devon. They sat on the couch and Mrs. Nelson paced.

"He had been married before, and now I know why it didn't last. They had a son, too, and his wife got custody. Franklin swore it wouldn't happen again, and I guess he figured the safest way to make sure I didn't get custody was to make me afraid to divorce him, and to keep me away from my son from the beginning.

"I wasn't allowed to take care of my son, ever." She stopped pacing, looking at Becky, her face tragic. "He said if I ever tried to leave, he would manufacture evidence to put me in jail and make sure I never saw Devon again. I was afraid . . . of my own husband!"

Becky and Devon sat totally still, Devon evidently mesmerized by the drama in his mother's voice. He probably thinks she's telling him a story, Becky thought.

"I left everything behind," Mrs. Nelson went on. "The first chance I had, I ran. I was taking Devon to a photo session at Franklin's mother's house, and we had to stop by the tailor's for a final fitting on Devon's jacket. Devon's nursemaid became ill at the last minute and didn't come, so I was alone except for the chauffeur. When the tailor went to ready the fitting room for Devon, I just . . . I grabbed him and ran out the back door. The chauffeur was out front.

"I guess I had already decided to leave without

knowing I'd decided, if that makes any sense. And when I saw my chance, I took it. I went to the bank and withdrew all I could and ran, leaving everything behind.

"See" — Mrs. Nelson had to pause to blow her nose — "See, there'd been a . . . what do you call it? A last straw. The package I got from my mother."

She took a deep breath and held her chin higher, determined to finish her story. "My father died when I was little. Just before I married Franklin, my mother finally remarried. She and her new husband moved into a smaller house.

"I had left my childhood doll collection at my mother's house, and she didn't have room to store it anymore, so she packed it up and sent it to me. Franklin was home when the box arrived. I guess he didn't recognize my mother's new return address — she hadn't put her name on the box — and he was convinced it was a gift to me — from a man.

"When I came home, he was in a rage. He was throwing my dolls around the room, smashing them." She covered her face with her hands. "It was awful! My grandmother had given me her doll — an antique Southern Belle with porcelain hands and head. She was shattered. Ruined. It was the last straw."

Mrs. Nelson looked up, dry-eyed, but haunted. "I didn't let Franklin see how upset I was, but that was the moment I must have decided to leave him.

"I have friends from before I was married. One

of them knew your school counselor, and that's how I found you. I didn't dare advertise. Some of my friends live where Franklin has his offices, and I call them regularly to check on him. And I have friends here. They arranged for me to have this cabin. They watch the marina and the boatyard. They watch the hotels and restaurants. We're all watching . . . for him.

"One of these days, he's going to show up."

When Mrs. Nelson finished her story, she simply sat, staring at Becky. After a few moments of silence, Devon started squirming.

"I'd better go fix dinner," Becky said. "He likes to help me. It'll keep him occupied. Would you like some tea or something?"

Mrs. Nelson shook her head silently. Her face was still pale, and pleading.

"I do understand," Becky said, answering the pleading look. "Everything makes a lot more sense now." She hugged the baby tightly, thinking that she and Devon both were in the middle of a mess . . . with no way out.

Chapter 18

Becky opened Devon's window but left his shade down with a four-inch gap at the bottom where she could look in to check on him.

She took down the play screen, folded it back in accordion-type folds, and leaned it up against the cabin near the baby's window. Then she carried the lounge chair about twenty feet from the house, arranging it so that only her legs would be in the sun.

Mrs. Nelson had stopped by the library for her, so Becky chose a murder mystery and carried it, a towel, and a huge glass of iced suntea out to the lounge chair.

With the towel between her and the plastic seat, a book, the hot sun, and a cold drink — and Devon sleeping peacefully — Becky was ready in either case . . . in case Cleve stopped by, and in case he didn't.

She thought about Mrs. Nelson's story, still not certain how she felt about it. I'm angry, she thought. Angry that Mrs. Nelson put me in the middle of this without telling me. And I'm worried that Mr. Nelson will find her and try to take Devon. I'm a little afraid, too. It could get ugly if he shows up.

I thought this would be romantic, she admitted to herself. Keeping an eye on a poor little rich boy, living on a beautiful, remote island, making a ton of money for helping keep a little boy safe . . . it sounded romantic.

Instead, I'm in the middle of a messy divorce, stuck in a little cabin every day. There's a town, but I can't go to it. There's a phone, but I can't use it. I can't mingle with any of the people or enjoy the island. I can't even get to know Cleve well enough to decide whether he's a spy or a possible romance. He keeps inviting me out for a sail, and right now, I'm so desperate for something different, I think I'd even do it! Well, maybe I would.

She opened her book, but before she could get engrossed in it she heard the sound of twigs crackling, and then Cleve calling hello. She was glad — that was why she'd come out, hoping he would stop by — but she was also curious and slightly uneasy again.

He has that effect on me, she thought. I'm never quite sure about him. How does he always see me out here? There's nothing but trees between here and his place. Does he sit at home with binoculars?

"Hi," he said. "Are you ready for that sail?"

I'd like to see the harbor, anyway, she thought. I'd maybe even get into the boat . . . at the dock. She sighed.

"I take it that means no?"

"I can't," Becky said.

"A walk? Care to go see if the whales are running?"

Becky shook her head.

"A swim?"

"I can't, Cleve."

"Are you a prisoner here?" he asked. "Can you meet me in town tonight?"

"I'll ask," Becky told him. "But . . . I wouldn't count on it."

Cleve gave her another of his odd stares. "If you're not interested, you could just say no," he said.

Becky didn't know what to say, but she knew she had to tell him something.

"I'm not supposed to say anything," she finally said. "But I'm working for my aunt. It's a confidential job, and I can't tell you anything about it, but she's paying me generously to give up my summer. I'm supposed to be available twenty-four hours a day. I'm enjoying the job, but it doesn't leave me much free time, and I can't ever predict when I'll have time off."

It may be incomplete, but it's all I can tell him, she thought. She felt guilty giving him that much information, but the expression on his face had softened, and she was relieved.

"All I can promise you is when I do have time off, I'll try to get into town and see you."

He smiled slowly, accepting the story, then his smile broadened into a grin. "About the other night," he said.

Becky knew he was talking about the pacifier. She felt her face heat up. "It belongs to my littlest brother," she said, looking at him defiantly, daring him to tease her. "He loves to put things in my purse, and I guess he dropped that in before I left. I have so much stuff in there, I didn't notice. . . ."

Devon, you are certainly making my life difficult, she thought, watching the amusement on Cleve's face. As she watched, his eyes roamed the clearing around the cabin, then narrowed, looking back at her. His expression was odd.

She wondered what he was thinking now, what had made his amusement fade. "I can give you some real money," she said. "For the chowder. But I'm not paying for the bread. You ate most of that, anyway."

"Your little brother's, huh?" Cleve's eyes looked beyond her again, toward the house. "I suppose you're going to tell me that's his, too?"

Becky turned around, following his gaze, but she didn't see anything. She turned to look at Cleve. He was giving her another of his famous odd looks.

"What are you talking about?" she asked.

"That," Cleve said, pointing towards Devon's window.

Chapter 19

Oh, no. Becky could feel her heart thumping in fear. He didn't see Devon. He couldn't have.

He's pointing at something else.

She looked again and saw a small, tan teddy bear tangled in a bush outside of Devon's window.

Oops.

Cleve laughed at her expression.

"It's mine," Becky said, her face burning again. She remembered playing toss with Devon, tossing the teddy bear for him to catch. He'd scrambled after the wild throws, giggling, enjoying the experience of being outside.

Devon tripped, Becky thought. Chasing it that last time. So I washed him up, fed him lunch, and put him down for his nap. I must not have noticed the bear when I folded up the screen.

"His name is Franklin," she said quickly.

"You brought your teddy bear with you on vacation?"

"Yes." Becky hoped she sounded convincing,

even though she could think of a lot of things she'd rather do with Cleve than try to convince him she took her teddy bear with her everywhere she went.

"I've had him a long time," she said, trying to smile. "He sleeps on my bed at home. I couldn't bear to leave him behind."

"That was a pun," Cleve said, his eyes glinting with humor. "Couldn't bear to leave the bear behind."

Becky looked at him, trying to decide whether he thought she was totally nuts or only partially nuts.

"What's the bear doing out here?" Cleve asked.

He thinks I'm nuts, Becky decided. He probably thinks I carry it around with me. "He's working on his tan," Becky said.

"I see." Cleve's look of amusement hadn't faded.

He's not going to let it drop, she thought. Well, I deserve it. I should have been more careful. Mrs. Nelson would have a fit if she knew anyone had seen Devon's teddy. "How's Calvin?" she asked. "Have you heard anything?"

Cleve's expression changed to relief. "I called him at the hospital," he said. "He's doing much better. They operated, and they think he should regain almost full use of the ankle. They said maybe a slight limp, and maybe not even that."

"I'm glad," Becky said.

Cleve nodded. "Me, too," he said softly. "He rambled a little. I think he's on pain pills. But he sounded okay." He grinned again. "I noticed your change of subject," he said. "I think it's kind of sweet that you brought your teddy bear."

Becky punched him on the arm. "You leave my teddy bear out of this," she ordered. "If you tease me, I swear I'll have him beat you up. He's pretty ferocious."

"So I'd better watch out for Franklin, huh?"

I don't know about you, Becky thought. But I'm going to watch out for Franklin! And I don't mean the teddy bear.

After Cleve left, Becky carried the bear inside, searching carefully for anything else she might have left outside. She wondered if Devon had had an old teddy bear that he loved, if he loved his new one as much. She wondered if a new teddy bear worked as well as an old one for cuddling at night, for making him feel less alone and more secure.

Mrs. Nelson came home looking grave. "Did you know a teenager named Cleve pushed the sheriff off a cliff?" she asked. "The whole town's been talking about it. And he lives right down the hill from us. He's the one you saw out for the walk that day, isn't he? The day the washer and dryer came."

"I heard about the sheriff," Becky said, stung by Cleve being blamed. "I heard about it the night it happened. Only I heard he fell."

"He was an expert climber," Mrs. Nelson said. "He couldn't fall. Cleve was with him, and he must have pushed him. The only question is why."

"If anyone actually thought Cleve had pushed the sheriff, he'd have been arrested," Becky said.

"By whom?" Mrs. Nelson asked pointedly. "With the sheriff out of the way, there's no one to arrest anyone. There's no one in authority on the island."

"It's just gossip," Becky insisted.

"I hope you're right," Mrs. Nelson said. "I'm just so worried about those phone calls you keep getting that I can't think straight. Isn't it odd that whoever is calling only calls while I'm gone? I mean, how do they know I'm gone? I'm afraid, Becky. I'm afraid he's found me."

"But you said you were watching the ferries!" Becky carried the chef salad and hard rolls to the table. "You said you'd see him if he came." She brought over Devon's warming trays.

Mrs. Nelson started feeding her son. "He hasn't come on the ferries," she said. "But he could have hired a boat. If you have a boat, you can get on the island without anyone knowing."

Devon seemed to catch the intensity of the conversation, fussing more than usual, pushing his mother's hand away and turning his head.

"But he couldn't hide here for long," Becky said. "He has to sleep somewhere, and eat. Even if he's staying on a boat, people will see him. The marina people watch the boats. They know what's going on. And you said you had people everywhere, helping you watch."

"Devon's so fussy this time of day," Mrs. Nelson said. She turned the job over to Becky and sat, staring at her own food. "My friends say he hasn't been at any of his offices lately," Mrs. Nelson said, giving Becky a distracted glance. "I made careful phone arrangements so no one would have this number. If anyone needs to call me, they call one certain friend of mine and she gets a message to me when I go to town. I didn't want to be traced. That one friend is the only person other than me who has this phone number, but she hasn't called. I asked."

Becky stirred, momentarily ignoring Devon. "Then . . . "

"The phone calls can't be good news," Mrs. Nelson said. "What if someone found out your name? Found out I hired you? Then they could find us through the number. Maybe it wasn't so smart to put everything in your name after all. I thought he couldn't trace me that way, but maybe I left an easy trail."

"But if he was here, wouldn't he do more than just call?"

"He would. He will. I don't think he's here yet." Mrs. Nelson actually crossed her fingers. "But I think he got the phone number. I think he's the one calling, trying to get you to answer. And since he only calls when I'm gone, somehow he knows when you're here alone. How could he know that unless he's got someone local on his payroll? And isn't it just too coincidental that the sheriff isn't here to help us if we need him? You can see why I'm so worried."

Becky shuddered. One person has been around here a lot, she thought. Just one.

Mrs. Nelson smiled.

Chapter 20

How can she smile about it? Becky thought. She may seem tense and nervous, but she must be a rock inside. Here I am shivering, and I'm not even the one in danger.

I'm not the one in danger.

At first the thought was comforting. She finished feeding Devon and washed his hands and face, admiring Mrs. Nelson's calmness.

But when Becky put Devon to bed that night and the noises of the evening started — the wind rushing through the tall firs, the chattering of birds as they settled into their sleeping places — the thought of danger reaching into the little cabin grew.

I'm not the one in danger.

But if Devon is in danger, I am, too. I'm in danger because if someone tries to take Devon, they'll have to get by me first.

If anyone is spying on Mrs. Nelson, he's spying on me, too.

Becky suddenly felt cooped up. The windows of the cabin were eyes, only instead of looking out at the world, they looked in at her. She felt exposed, like a target.

Becky kissed Devon and tucked his teddy bear — the same one she'd claimed as her own and named Franklin — a little more firmly into his arms. She made certain the drapes and shades were closed and went to the living room where she'd left her books.

She was surprised to see Mrs. Nelson curled up on the couch, barefoot, reading.

"Oh," she said when she noticed Becky. "I hope you don't mind that I borrowed a book. I used to read all the time."

Before Devon? Becky wondered. Or before you got married? "Is it any good?" she asked.

"Riveting, actually," Mrs. Nelson admitted. "I was only going to skim the first chapter and I couldn't put it down."

She turned back to her reading and Becky watched for a moment, uncertain whether to mention that Mrs. Nelson had chosen the book Becky had already started reading.

Then she realized what a rare opportunity had presented itself. And I almost missed it! Becky thought happily.

"As long as you're happy reading, I'm going for a walk," she said. "I'm going to the point to see if the whales are out."

Mrs. Nelson looked trapped, and Becky went on before she could think of an objection. "I've been dying to go to the point. This is a wonderful opportunity. I really appreciate it."

She hurried towards the kitchen. "I don't expect to be long," she called, grabbing her flashlight. "But this might be my only chance to see the whales, so if they're out, I may just stay and watch. Don't try to pick Devon up. That always wakes him. And if he's just making little whiney noises, don't turn the light on. He'll go back to sleep. Bye!"

She slipped out the door before Mrs. Nelson could answer and ran to the path Cleve had told her led to the point.

The clouds had spread lazily across the sky, and the sun, though low in the sky, was still hot. The path wound alongside the stream, in and out of small stands of trees, then through the denser growth with the ever-present firs towering like guardians over the smaller trees and ferny bushes. The light breeze smelled of salt.

At first, relieved to have escaped the cabin, Becky simply enjoyed the pleasure of walking alone through the woods, but Mrs. Nelson's comments about Cleve kept intruding on her peace.

She said everyone thinks Cleve pushed the sheriff, Becky remembered. That's ridiculous! He's been so worried about him.

Someone local is spying on us. Mrs. Nelson's words floated through her mind, then stuck like a lump in her throat.

Not Cleve.

Why not? Just because he's good-looking and

pays attention to me? Because he acts like he likes me?

I'm not such a great judge of character, Becky thought glumly. Jason's proof of that.

She'd reached the place where the path split, one direction following the stream, the other going to the point. Farther on, the path to the point split again, going right, almost straight down the cliffs to the water, or left, to a natural outcropping that stuck out like a pointing finger, overlooking the sea from a height of about one hundred yards.

Boniface, Becky thought. Babyface. She peered over the edge, but it made her feel dizzy to look straight down. She sat back a safe distance from the edge and leaned against a rock, watching out to sea for the dark shapes of whales.

I thought Jason loved me, she reminded herself. And all the time he was flirting with Sarah. Once he was sure Sarah was interested, he dropped me flat. Why should I believe Cleve will be any different?

Because I want him to be?

Part of her mind spoke up quietly, insisting Cleve *was* different. But the rest of her mind remembered the odd, constant questions about her "aunt" and the cabin, about their business. She remembered how he kept popping up at odd times, how he always seemed to know when she was outside, when she went to town, and his strange looks and sudden mood changes.

He could be spying on us, she thought.

But he never asks about a baby. Sometimes it seems like he's fishing for information, but not what I'd expect him to ask if he were looking for a baby.

Off in the distance, the rhythmic sweep of the water toward the shore was disturbed by a small boat cutting crosswise, coming closer, sending cross-ripples, and Becky recognized Cleve's boat.

Chapter 21

He waved and shouted, beckoning to her. He pointed to the path she hadn't taken, the one that led almost straight down to the sea.

I can't climb down that! Becky thought, shaking her head even though she knew he couldn't see the gesture from his boat.

Still, she'd leaned forward eagerly when she'd thought the boat was Cleve's, and she'd leapt to her feet, waving, when she'd been sure.

He might never have seen me if I hadn't jumped up, she thought. And since I waved, he thinks I was calling him over.

I guess I was calling him over. And I can't just wave him away now.

Maybe I wanted the chance to ask him a few questions, she thought. He should be able to tell his side of the story about Calvin.

She hadn't made a conscious decision, yet she found herself eyeing the path that led down the steep hillside, judging whether she could make it.

She walked over to the ladderlike beginning of the descent, shrouded to the right with trees, to the left with shadows. She looked down at the first few handholds and footholds. The first few were all she could see.

Don't look down, she told herself. Climb, but don't look, and you'll be fine. Just climb down and say hi from the ledge. You don't have to get in the boat.

She slid down into the hollowed-out semicircle at the top and turned around, holding a tree trunk with her right hand and feeling with her feet for the first step.

This is where the sheriff fell, she reminded herself. Cleve knows that. Maybe he knows the path is too steep for me and he figures I'll fall.

The thought startled her, and she paused.

Becky, she told herself firmly. Either you trust him, or you don't. You've been around Mrs. Nelson too long. Cleve didn't push the sheriff.

She felt for the next step, and the next.

After the first thirty feet or so, she found the going easier. The path was less steep, and the footholds and handholds more obvious . . . or else she was getting more adept at climbing.

Instead of a shoreline at the bottom, Becky climbed down to a ledge that formed a kind of natural pier. Is this the one the sheriff landed on? she wondered. She caught herself looking around for blood.

Cleve pulled his boat up next to her. "Climb in," he said.

"No." Becky shook her head. "I just climbed down to say hi. I don't want a ride."

"The whales are out." He pointed. "I know a perfect spot for watching. You can't miss this, Becky. It's a magnificent sight. How many times do you get to see a pod of orcas?"

I really do want to see the whales, Becky thought, her mouth dry. She took a deep breath, then scrambled into the boat before she could change her mind, her heart pounding, her hands clammy.

Cleve turned the sail to catch the breeze, and the boat leapt off.

He maneuvered expertly along the coastline. "We can't go too close," he said apologetically. "We'll worry them. There!" He pointed again, his face excited. "See? Dark spots. There."

Becky followed his pointing finger and saw the dark shapes moving through the water like semis on the highway — confident in their size and ability, unconcerned with the petty hurries and worries of the rest of the traffic.

Cleve turned the sail again and they sat in the water. They were near enough that Becky could sort the shapes into snouts and tails, big whales and babies — about twenty of them, Becky guessed — heading where instinct sent them.

Like me, Becky thought. Instinct made me want to get as far away from Jason and Sarah as I could, and now I'm here, watching whales who probably have a better reason for being here than I do.

"They travel in family pods," Cleve said. "They stay with their families forever. That's a big pod. Usually there're only a half-dozen or so. Did you know they use sonar?"

"Like bats?" Becky asked, trying not to think of all the water beneath her.

"Kind of. It's called echolocation. Underwater sonar, I guess, but they can tell a lot with it, even the density of the object in their path."

"Are they blind, then?"

Cleve shook his head, watching the whales. "Underwater, at least, they can see fine. That's why we don't want to go too close. If they see us, or echolocate us, they'll go away. Aren't they magnificent? How could anybody hunt them?"

Becky watched his face, excited and proud, as if the whales were his own creation. He loves them, she thought.

"They're called killer whales," Cleve said softly. "But they don't kill any more than the other whales. They have teeth, though, instead of baleen, so they look more ferocious. And they do eat sea mammals. They hunt cooperatively. Cooperation is a signal of something in animals. Some people argue that it means communication, some say higher intelligence and awareness, some say it's just pack instinct. Did you know the horse and the whale are supposedly descended from the same ancestor?"

"No," Becky murmured, enjoying Cleve's obvious pleasure in the whales. The rocking of the little boat would have been soothing except that she knew it was waves of water making it rock.

"No one knows why whales returned to the sea," Cleve said. He looked at her suddenly. "I'm lecturing. Sorry. I get like that."

"I'm interested," Becky told him.

"I often wonder why some animals stay in family packs," Cleve said, looking thoughtful. "Anthropologists argue that it isn't normal behavior, even for people. They say the older tribes of people traded children — like if they were going on a trip and didn't want to take a baby, they'd trade for an older child. The Romans just dumped babies they didn't want, and killed off inconvenient or tiresome relatives left and right. Family ties didn't mean much of anything. It's been said people probably didn't mate for life in a lot of cultures, and that might have been a good thing for the gene pool or something. So it surprises me to see animals stick together. Sometimes I think they're more advanced than we are."

They watched the pod of whales swim slowly by, enormous, peaceful, the babies straying from their mothers' sides, then swimming playfully back. Even from a distance they looked huge, like dinosaurs.

Killer whales, Becky thought. Would it be such a bad way to die — swallowed by a whale? It would be an innocent death. Not like murder at all. If a whale swallowed me, it would be because I was food, not because he wanted me to die. Why am I thinking about death? Because of killer whales and falling sheriffs? Or because I'm on the ocean and I'm afraid of it?

She stood gingerly, shading her eyes with her hands. Behind her she could see Cleve putting film in his camera. "So the sheriff's going to be fine?" she asked.

"Yeah. I hope they don't keep him on those pain pills too long. He was really wandering. Said some pretty strange stuff."

"Did he say how he fell?"

"Not exactly," Cleve said. He turned toward her, almost too quickly. Startled, Becky threw an arm up and suddenly, with no warning, she was falling, cracking her shin, her hip, falling overboard.

The terror was instantaneous as the cold, dark water closed over her, shrouding her. She felt swallowed, buried under miles and miles of lapping, sucking, crashing, crushing water.

The water closed over her head like the rain of dirt clods on a coffin. I can't swim, she thought.

Chapter 22

Can I float?

I can float, she told herself, pushing the panic back as if it were a curtain. Not very well with my shoes on, but I can do it.

She kicked, fighting the fear and the water, hoping she would go up and not down. Down meant seaweed, and green depths — a watery finish.

I almost passed beginners swimming, she thought. I learned to do a backfloat with a kick. I can do it. If I can get to the top, I can float.

It felt like forever, but she finally broke to the surface and took a deep breath, clumsily trying to get on top of the water. The last rays of the sun were shining in her eyes as it set, blinding her. Her clothes and shoes acted like weights, dragging at her, dragging her down.

Out of the corner of her eye she saw a whale coming toward her, mouth open, and despite what she'd thought earlier, being eaten by a whale seemed very personal.

No! was all she could think. Her fear made her thrash at the water, and she went down again, the waterlogged jeans and sneakers sucking her deep into murky, seaweedy fogs.

Her life began to flash in her mind . . . her instructor showing them how to tie knots in the legs of a pair of jeans and use them to capture air, to float with . . . Jason, his expression distant, polite, finally saying, "I think you're making too big a deal out of this, Becky. It happens all the time. People get tired of each other." Each flash was as complete as a dream.

Then she was breathing again. I saved Timmy, she thought. But he was in the wading pool. And I had a swimsuit on, not jeans. Take them off. That's what I have to do. Take them off. Take off my shoes.

But she couldn't do it; when she put her face in the water she started to sink, and she couldn't kick and grab her pantlegs at the same time. I have to do it, she thought, but the thought was no longer urgent as she sank again.

She flashed again . . . Timmy, bravely wiping tears from his eyes as she left for the summer. "I promise I'll watch Mike and we won't go in your room. Just come back okay?" . . .

. . . Cleve, his hands reaching towards her, pushing . . .

No. I made that up.

Eventually Becky realized she was choking. Choking on air.

Then she realized someone was calling her name.

She opened her eyes. She was in the boat. Cleve's boat. Stretched uncomfortably across the seat. A face loomed over her . . . Cleve's face, anxious and relieved.

"You're awake," he whispered. He wiped at his face with the back of his hand, looking very much like Timmy.

Becky sat up slowly, feeling surprisingly well. "I'm okay," she said.

Cleve blinked hard and then hugged her.

"You're getting wet," Becky said. "I'm soaked."

Cleve took his jacket off and wrapped it around her, his arm lingering on her shoulders.

"What happened?" Becky asked.

"I don't know. You leaned forward a little to look at the orcas, and I turned around to take a picture of you, and then you tumbled into the water. You must have lost your balance."

He looked at her, his face troubled. "Like Calvin," he said slowly.

Becky shivered. I was trying not to think that, she thought.

"Am I hexed?" Cleve asked, trying to smile. "Twice in a lifetime is too much. Twice within a few days is scary. Are you sure you're okay?"

Becky drew in a deep, shivery breath. "I'm okay," she said again.

"I was so scared!" Cleve told her. "The sun was in my eyes, and I was afraid I'd run you over if I had to move the boat. But I didn't know how well you could swim in your clothes. It's hard to swim in clothes. And I couldn't see you! And when I did see you, it looked as if you were going down for the second or third time. I thought you'd never grab the life ring."

I grabbed the ring? "Did . . . did a whale try to get me?"

As soon as she asked, Becky knew it was a stupid question. The whales were too far away. It was the boat. Cleve's boat. She'd seen the boat out of the corner of her eye . . . trying to run her down?

Trying to finish the job? No. He threw me a life ring.

Even after she was safe in bed and dry, and the shakes were gone, Becky still couldn't figure out what happened. Nobody pushed me, she told herself. I didn't feel anyone's hands on me. That was later, when he pulled me out of the water.

Cleve had wanted to take her to his place and dry her clothes, but Becky had refused. She'd dried out a lot on the walk back to the cabin, and managed to get into her own room without Mrs. Nelson seeing her. She'd called, "I'm back. Good-night." Mrs. Nelson had simply said good-night in return.

As she got ready for bed, she kept trying to put together the pieces of what had happened.

Cleve had been the only one there. Just like he had been the only one there when the sheriff went over.

Cleve said the sheriff is fine.

Mrs. Nelson says Cleve should be arrested and that everyone thinks he pushed the sheriff over the cliff.

Someone is lying, or is deliberately trying to confuse me.

Who? And why?

Chapter 23

"I have evening meetings all this week," Mrs. Nelson said.

Don't plan on leaving, Becky translated. No time off.

"I haven't heard any good news about the sheriff," Mrs. Nelson went on. "I heard he's in a coma and might not wake up from it. There are people who think we need to call in the FBI or something." She checked her face in the mirror and grabbed her purse. "It's already July," she said, opening the front door. "I can't believe how fast . . . "

She screamed.

Becky, frozen, felt like she was underwater again, too heavy, too . . . sinking.

She ran to the door and stared down at the porch, feeling numb, yet still horrified. She would have screamed, too, except that Mrs. Nelson was doing a good enough job for both of them.

Chapter 24

The doll was smashed.

Becky looked at the head. It was a thousand little pieces, yet the body was whole, lying like a miniature abandoned child . . . a horribly mutilated child.

One painted blue eye stared at Becky, accusing.

"It's him," Mrs. Nelson said, her face white and her eyes staring blankly at the shattered doll. "He's here. He found us."

Us!

She means her and Devon, Becky told herself, but no matter how Becky looked at the situation, *us* included her, too.

Mrs. Nelson turned to Becky, grabbing her arms with a frantic grip. "Don't let him take Devon away from me! Help me. Please!"

Becky wanted to pull free of Mrs. Nelson's grasp, wanted to run away from Mrs. Nelson's problems, from her nagging doubts about Cleve, from the broken doll.

She patted her boss soothingly. "Go make some tea," she suggested with a calmness she did not feel. "Check on Devon. Make sure the screaming didn't wake him. I'll clean up this mess. Then we'll talk. We'll figure out something."

She swallowed hard as she swept up the blue eye. It's a message, she thought. *I'm after you. I found you. This is what you'll look like when I'm done with you.*

She glanced a. ound, suddenly afraid. Is someone watching me now?

The forest looked full of eerily misshapen trees, the shadows threatening. The safe little cabin seemed dim and mysterious, and very isolated . . . though not isolated from danger.

When she stepped back inside, even the cabin walls seemed infused with darkly whispered secrets.

Becky tossed the swept-up doll into the trash. This is the work of a sick mind, she thought. Mrs. Nelson made tea, and Becky joined her at the table, absently stirring the tea in her cup. "I thought he couldn't get here without someone telling you," she said.

Mrs. Nelson didn't answer. She was staring blankly at nothing.

"If someone had seen him, they'd have let you know," Becky said. "That's what you told me. They'd see him at the marina, the boatyard, the hotels. They'd see him if he rented a car, or if he walked through town. Isn't that right?"

"I guess so. But who else could it be?"

Who? Becky thought. "Who else knew about the dolls?"

"I didn't tell anyone about that. Just you."

"Are you sure?" Becky asked. "You could have let it slip into a conversation without noticing, couldn't you? That happens sometimes. How about when you arranged for your friend to hire me? Or arranged to have this place rented? You might have mentioned it to someone."

Mrs. Nelson shook her head. "I wasn't brought up to publicly discuss private things. It was difficult enough to tell you, and I remember every word I said. I remember what I told my friends, too. The only other person involved is John Hillyer. He's helping us watch, but I didn't explain anything to him . . . not about that."

"Would your husband have told anyone?"

"Oh, no!" Mrs. Nelson looked almost amused. "He would never admit he'd done anything like that. He thought he was perfect. Besides, he didn't really have anyone he talked to about personal things. His friends were all business friends."

Becky drank her tea, drumming the fingers of her other hand on the table. The rhythm helped her think. "What you're saying is, the only person who could have done that to the doll is your husband, yet he couldn't have done it because you have people watching, and they would have seen him if he were here."

Mrs. Nelson nodded. "But he didn't have to put

the doll there himself," she pointed out. "He could have hired someone else to do it for him. He didn't have to explain why if he paid enough."

The evidence is mounting, Becky thought. But I don't believe it. It couldn't be Cleve. But his story doesn't match up. Cleve said he talked to the sheriff. Mrs. Nelson said she heard the sheriff's in a coma and might not wake up. I don't have enough information!

Maybe it's Mr. Hillyer, or one of her other friends. They're more involved in Mrs. Nelson's life than Cleve is. They could have lied to her about the sheriff. Actually, it could be anyone.

"Well," Becky said finally. "If your husband hired someone else to do this, we have two problems. One is, we're being spied on. And the other problem is, I don't think your husband is going to be happy making phone calls that no one answers, and hiring someone to smash dolls."

Becky looked sideways at her boss. "He's going to come," she said. "We'll just have to be ready."

Chapter 25

Becky folded laundry, wondering how her boss was doing on her rounds. Mrs. Nelson had explained her system — her friends kept track of everyone who arrived on the island who could possibly be Mr. Nelson. They told Mrs. Nelson, and she went to find the suspects and look at them herself.

Becky sighed, listening automatically for Devon as she stacked clothes. I have to come up with a plan, she told herself. One she'll approve of. She's found something wrong with everything I've thought of so far.

Becky had suggested taking the baby to her own house and watching him there, but Mrs. Nelson wouldn't hear of it. "I won't let him out of my sight!" she'd said. "I wouldn't be able to sleep. I didn't go through all this trouble just to send him off somewhere without me."

Then Becky had suggested they both leave and take the baby somewhere else. "He'll have thought of that," Mrs. Nelson had said. "He'll have someone ready to follow if I leave."

Becky had also suggested that Mrs. Nelson leave the island with a baby-shaped bundle, pretending she had Devon. "Then Devon and I will go wherever you want us to, and you can join us as soon as you've lost whoever follows you."

Mrs. Nelson had vetoed that as too risky. "I might not recognize whoever he hires to follow me," she'd said. "I'd wind up leading them straight to you and Devon."

Becky carried Devon's clothes to his room and put them away quietly.

Then we just have to sit here like ducks, she thought grimly. And wait for him to show up. What good is that going to do?

She carried her own clothing to her room, surprised to find her door shut.

I left it open, she thought. I know I did. I remember because the breeze felt so good, and I thought it would freshen the house. Oh, of course. The breeze. It must have blown the door shut. It's noisy in the utility room. I might not have heard. I'm lucky it didn't wake Devon.

She realized she'd been standing in the narrow hall for a full minute with the laundry in one hand and one hand on the knob to her door while she mentally convinced herself it was okay to open it.

I am in no danger, she told herself. Mr. Nelson isn't here yet, and whoever is spying . . . it can't be Cleve, but whoever it is, is just spying. Just watching the house. From the outside.

Still she hesitated.

Devon will wake up any minute now, she thought, turning the knob. I have to get my work done.

She pushed the door, feeling a slight resistance.

The wind, she told herself.

As she eased the door open she could feel the breeze around it, and relieved, she pushed it open all the way, peering quickly in.

She hadn't realized how edgy she was until she felt her shoulders sag in relief at the sight of her room — normal and undisturbed, the curtains billowing in the wind.

She dropped her laundry on the bed and closed the window, latching it, but the last bit of wind had already caught the door and it slammed shut behind her.

She yelped, jumping, then felt like an idiot. She turned around calmly, then screamed.

The doll was behind her door, a twin to the first. This doll's head had only one small piece broken out, but the body was hacked and slashed. Both innocent blue eyes stared at her, looking dismayed, as if begging Becky to explain what had happened to it.

It's a good thing dolls don't bleed, Becky thought dumbly.

Chapter 26

She'd stopped screaming almost immediately, afraid of disturbing Devon, but her breath came in ragged gasps.

Poor lifeless little thing, she thought.

No! It's a doll. It's not dead because it was never alive.

Devon called out and Becky jumped again.

"Bee-bee!" he called. "Up!"

"Okay, sweetie," Becky called back, amazed at how controlled her voice sounded. "Just a minute."

She grabbed the doll by one hacked leg and tossed it into the trash, tied the trash bag shut, and carried it with her to get Devon out of bed. She threw the bag into the big bin in the kitchen and started fixing a snack for the baby.

Her eyes kept snaking toward the trash, expecting a hacked little hand to reach out in a mutilated plea.

It's getting bizarre, she thought, strapping

Devon into his high chair. Someone was in the house!

No.

She snapped a bib around his neck. If someone threw the doll through the window, it could have hit the door. That's how it broke its head. The broken piece was there, too, beside the doll.

The more she thought about it, the better the theory sounded. It was a small relief to know the doll could have gotten into her room without a person getting in, too.

But only a small relief.

It's not amusing, Becky thought. Even if someone offered to pay me, I wouldn't do something like that.

Am I in danger?

She'd been trying not to ask that question since Mrs. Nelson had told her story, but the question kept asking itself anyway.

Am I in danger? Is Devon in danger?

She looked around the kitchen and it seemed small and unprotected. It seemed different, somehow . . . denser, thicker with something . . . some kind of guilty knowledge. Had something happened in here once, something evil? Something that stained the walls themselves with guilt?

Or was something going to happen?

Becky shivered, then smiled nervously at Devon. "I'm going nuts," she told him. "It's okay, though. Don't you worry. I'm going to take care of you."

I have to take care of him, Becky thought. His

mother doesn't know how, and his father . . . what about his father?

I'd been thinking that if Mr. Nelson showed up, all I'd have to worry about was getting Devon out of the way while they fought it out. I was thinking arguments, shouting . . . but not danger. Not real danger like slashed and broken . . . this is definitely sick.

But is it just some kind of sick humor, or is it dangerous sick? Maybe I should have taken psychology.

Devon started whining.

He fussed all afternoon in response to Becky's worried musings.

It didn't help that his mother arrived home pale and silent, carrying a new hat, and also carrying its box . . . separately from the hat.

Mrs. Nelson slammed the box on the counter where it loomed starkly, an alien thing squatting on its perch, watching and waiting while they ate dinner.

Becky and Mrs. Nelson ate silently, giving each other meaning-filled glances.

Devon fussed. He called again and again, "Mama, Bee-bee, Da-da," but pushed Becky and Mrs. Nelson away.

"He knows something's wrong," Becky whispered. "Babies always do."

"I don't think . . ." Mrs. Nelson began crisply, but her gaze strayed to the box, and she fell silent.

"We have to do something," Becky said. "We

can't stand much more of this. What about the police? Aren't the dolls evidence?"

"In case you've forgotten, someone managed to dispose of the sheriff," Mrs. Nelson said. "And besides, there's nothing illegal about leaving a doll on a front porch. Or on the front seat of a car." She nodded toward the box on the counter.

"Or tossing one through an open bedroom window," Becky added. Three, she thought. One in the car, too.

Mrs. Nelson sighed, pressing her hands against her forehead. "It's so ugly," she said.

Becky's gaze kept returning to the hat box, drawn again and again. She didn't want to think about it, but her mind kept painting pictures . . . slashed dolls, burned dolls, beheaded dolls. Finally she stood and marched to the counter.

Behind her Mrs. Nelson said, "Don't."

Becky slid the lid off the box.

She'd known it would be a doll, and she'd known it would be mutilated, but still the sight was shocking — the staring, accusing blue eyes, and the arms and legs, ripped from the body and lying in awkward, unnatural positions.

She gasped, thinking of drooling madmen with bloody axes, thinking of every horror movie she'd ever seen.

She put the lid back on. "The one in my room was hacked up," she said. "Sliced. Slashed. I don't know which is worse."

Devon quit fussing and started crying.

"Just get him to sleep!" Mrs. Nelson snapped. "I can't stand this. I'll do the dishes. Just get him out of here."

She's really upset! Becky thought, gathering Devon into her arms. He struggled and cried, but as Becky carried him to his room, then paced back and forth, singing softly, he gradually calmed himself, and gradually fell asleep.

I didn't change your diaper, Becky thought, putting him in his crib. I didn't put your pajamas on. It'll have to do. I won't chance waking you up.

She ran her finger softly over his face, tracing the pudgy line of his cheeks, and knew that she would do anything to make sure he was safe.

"We have to have a plan," Becky told Mrs. Nelson firmly. "I don't care if you don't like it, we have to have something! We can't come up with something foolproof, but we can come up with something. And that's better than sitting here feeling like the bull's-eye on a target!"

To her surprise, Mrs. Nelson nodded.

"If Mr. Nelson has found you, you have to leave," Becky said.

"But . . ."

"No buts. You have to go somewhere else. He might find you again, but it'll take awhile. Meanwhile, you've got a lawyer working on the divorce, right?"

Mrs. Nelson nodded.

"Get him to file one of those orders . . . restraining orders, aren't they?"

"What do you mean?" Mrs. Nelson wiped her eyes with a tissue.

"If he never did anything, you couldn't prove he was bothering you," Becky said. "But if he followed you here, that's evidence that he is bothering you, and you can get a court order saying he has to stay away."

Mrs. Nelson looked hopeful.

"The problem is," Becky went on, "that means we have to sit and wait for him to show up. What's the worst he would do?"

"Take my baby," Mrs. Nelson said fiercely.

Becky couldn't help remembering how Mrs. Nelson had ordered her to take the fussing Devon away. *She'll have a bit of a surprise when she gets into full-time baby care!* Becky thought.

"No, I mean, would he hurt you? Will he snatch Devon right out of your arms?" *Do I have to be afraid?*

"He hit things," Mrs. Nelson said slowly. "Smashed them. Burned them. But he never hit me or the baby. But I never took the baby and ran, either."

A new circumstance, Becky thought. That means we don't know what he'll do.

She was not reassured.

I guess I have to be afraid, she thought.

Chapter 27

But I'm not going to act like I'm afraid, Becky told herself, carrying the lawn chair, towel, book, and glass of iced tea out to her usual spot.

It had taken half the night, but they'd hammered out a plan.

They'd figured Mr. Nelson would come soon — within a day or two — and Mrs. Nelson had finally agreed that she would go stay with her mother and her mother's new husband, even if it meant imposing on newlyweds.

"Devon is more important," Becky had insisted, and Mrs. Nelson had seen the truth of her argument.

Becky had crept out in the night without a light and had hidden Devon's playpen in the dense fir stand between their cabin and Cleve's — back from the path Cleve would logically use.

"There's a kind of brandy that makes Franklin terribly sleepy," Mrs. Nelson said. "I'll get some in town. When he shows up, I'll get him to come inside to talk and I'll give him a glass of brandy. I don't think he realizes how sleepy he gets, so he'll drink it. You take Devon and go to the playpen the second he shows up. Wait with him thirty minutes. That'll give Franklin time to get tired.

"After exactly thirty minutes, you head back here. I'll be on my way to the playpen. If we coordinate the time we leave to change places, we won't be leaving the baby or Franklin alone for more than a couple of minutes. I'll arrange a boat to take me and Devon to Friday Harbor and we'll be on a ferry and gone before he wakes up enough to chase us.

"Franklin should sleep for hours, but if you'll wait with him one hour, that'll be enough. You can pack while you're waiting, and . . . go home, I guess. You have your return ticket. I'll give you a check before you go."

It's not a perfect plan, Becky thought, arranging her things. What if Mr. Nelson doesn't drink the brandy . . . if I can't get away fast enough . . . if he comes while Mrs. Nelson is gone. . . .

But it's better than no plan. I wish we could leave now, but it's too risky. We might not recognize whoever follows us, and they wouldn't have any problem snatching Devon if we didn't know who to watch out for. Is he watching now?

Becky shivered and eyed the woods surrounding her. The trees reached so far into the sky that they dwarfed the cabin, dwarfed her. They loomed above her. The cool depths of the forest made perfect hiding places for any number of watchers.

But who's watching?

She listened carefully, peering into the trees.

If I knew who it was . . .

The forest sighed, shifting restlessly, whispering.

Stop it! Becky told herself. Stop imagining, and think. If someone is watching, will Mr. Nelson call him off once he gets here? Or will we have the hidden watcher to worry about, too?

No . . . Becky shook her head. Whatever he's planning to do, I'm going to guess he won't want the watcher to see. Mrs. Nelson said he thinks he's perfect. He wouldn't want anyone else to see him taking Devon. He wouldn't chance having someone who could testify against him in court.

Of course, I'm guessing. And if he doesn't want any witnesses, how about me?

I'm a witness.

Chilled, Becky gathered her things and hurried back to the cabin. Even though she'd locked Devon in, she still checked every corner and closet looking for watchers or dolls or anything suspicious . . . feeling only slightly relieved when she found nothing.

I wish Cleve had stopped by when I was outside, she thought. I may not see him again. When Mr. Nelson comes, we have to run. I won't have time for good-byes.

Do I want to see him again? Is he the watcher?

She remembered Cleve's kiss, soft, warm, and uncomplicated.

Then she remembered Jason's kisses. They'd felt much the same way, and the next day she'd seen him kissing her best friend.

So much for love, she thought. I trusted Jason. I trusted Sarah. I think maybe my judgment isn't all that great. Maybe I should be glad Cleve didn't stop by.

She didn't feel glad.

She made sure the doors were locked again, then sat in Devon's room, watching, making sure he was safe.

Is he in danger? Will his father hurt him?

If there's been no divorce yet, Mrs. Nelson hasn't kidnapped her son because there are no custody orders. And if Mr. Nelson takes him, he won't be kidnapping him, either.

If no one is breaking any laws, the law can't help. Even if we had a sheriff, he couldn't do anything.

But Mr. Nelson doesn't sound normal. It isn't normal to burn someone's past or smash a doll collection . . . or leave mutilated dolls around to scare us half to death. It's sick.

I don't want to be in the middle of this, Becky thought, looking out the window at the forest, wondering if someone was out there, watching her. I don't feel safe. I'm afraid.

She dropped her glance, her eyes wandering to the corner where Devon's toys were stacked. I'm afraid of angry husbands and watchers in the woods. I'm afraid our plan isn't very good. And I'm afraid of sick minds. Disturbed people don't have the same stopping mechanisms inside that the rest of us do. They don't quit at the usual places. They go further.

She swallowed, wishing she had someone she could turn to for help. She felt the hairs on the back of her neck tickling and knew someone was watching her. She raised her head slowly, unwilling to look, not sure she wanted to see.

Chapter 28

She lifted her eyes to the window. There was no one there.

But the feeling of being stared at didn't go away.

Behind her Devon chuckled, and Becky nearly fainted in relief.

It was just the baby! she thought, turning around. Devon sat in his crib, watching her. In his arms, instead of the teddy bear Becky had named Franklin after his father . . . Devon held a doll.

Another one of *the* dolls.

Becky covered her mouth with her hand, staring at him. How did he get it?

This doll was perfect — no slashes, no broken, shattered head, no ripped limbs — and somehow it was even more frightening.

Almost like it's a fill-in-the-blank threat, Becky thought. Fill it in with anything I can imagine.

The doll, its blue eyes staring at her innocently, looked as angelic and pink-cheeked as Devon did.

"Bee-Bee? Up!" Devon said. He dropped the doll through the crib slats onto the floor, pulled himself up, and held his arms out over the railing. "Up?" he pleaded.

Is he in danger? Is his father a dangerous man? What will he do to witnesses he doesn't want around?

Becky kicked the doll under the crib. She heard it hit the wall and wondered if its head had survived intact.

"Life would be a lot simpler if people could just get along," she told Devon as she lifted him from his crib. "Your parents had money, good jobs, and a beautiful baby."

"Ba-by," Devon said, patting himself on the stomach.

Becky smiled at him. "Yes, you," she said, grabbing a fresh diaper to put on him. "But look what happened. You don't have a father, you don't have a home, you and your mom are hiding out with only a teenaged baby-sitter to protect you . . . and I don't think I'm all that great at this kind of rescuing. To be perfectly honest, I'm scared. I'm in the middle of a mess and I'm afraid. And besides all that, I don't even know if I can trust the guy I'm fall- ing . . ."

She broke off suddenly, startled at what she'd almost said. *The guy I'm falling in love with.*

"Oh, no!" she said, finishing the diaper change. "I'm nuts. I'm totally crazy! I don't even know if he

tried to kill me . . . and the sheriff. He's possibly
. . . probably? working for your father, doing sick
things to scare us, and I'm . . ."

She shook her head, then her eyes strayed to the
doll under Devon's bed.

The doll.

"I need time to think!" she said.

Devon looked serious, mimicking her mood.

"I know I could figure out what to do if I just
had time to think about it!" she said.

The phone rang.

"No!" Becky screamed, and Devon started
crying.

"I quit!" Becky said. "I didn't sign on for dead
dolls and telephones that won't quit ringing. I
signed on to baby-sit. That's all! Just to baby-sit
and do housework. I'm supposed to be a mother's
summer helper. If this is what it's like to be a mother's helper, I quit!"

She gave Devon a snack, but he didn't eat it. The
phone jangled at both of them. When it quit, she
and Devon both laughed and it sounded to Becky
like borderline hysteria.

Do babies get hysterical?

When the phone started again, Becky marched
over, picked the lock, and disconnected the phone
wire.

"She can't fire me because I already quit!" she
said.

Time dragged.

The afternoon lasted forever.

Finally Becky set up the play screen and took Devon outside. What could it hurt? she asked herself. If someone's watching, they already know we're here.

She tried to play games with the baby, but her attention was on the doll under Devon's bed, and on Cleve.

All those odd questions, she thought. Hanging around. Watching, watching. Is he the watcher? *Does your boss have her own income? Crime never pays. . . .*

Wait a minute! she thought. *Does your boss have her own credit rating? Her own income? Why would anyone sign a contract at 17 if they knew it wasn't valid?* How did he know? He knew the phone and the cabin were in my name and not in Mrs. Nelson's! That's why he was asking those questions. How did he know?

Is he the one who's calling?

The phone rang.

Becky and Devon both froze. The sound reached them clearly, even outside in Devon's play yard.

It can't be ringing! Becky thought, grabbing Devon and holding him to her. I disconnected it!

Chapter 29

The phone was definitely ringing.

It was not Becky's imagination.

She checked. It was plugged in. And ringing. It was definitely ringing.

She unplugged it again. This time she unplugged the wire from the wall and from the phone and put the wire in her pocket.

Then she checked the doors and windows again.

The front door was unlocked.

Becky remembered locking it. She remembered checking it, and double-checking it.

Could I have unlocked it, thinking I was locking it?

I don't know.

I don't know anything anymore.

Chapter 30

"Because I'm not the hero type!" Becky told Mrs. Nelson.

Her boss had not come home at her usual time. She hadn't come home for dinner. She hadn't come home until Devon was asleep, and when she did arrive, the first thing Becky had done was say, "I quit!

"I can handle all the usual things like colds and bloody noses!" Becky went on, not waiting for Mrs. Nelson to say anything. "I've taken care of three little brothers and a whole ton of other children. I've taken baby-sitting courses. I'm prepared! I can handle babies spitting up, and fevers, and skinned knees. I can even rescue little ones from wading pools and comfort them while they get stitches. But I can't handle this!

"This isn't the usual stuff at all! I can work twelve-hour days. I can entertain a one-year-old. I can read *Colors and Numbers* two hundred times. I can change diapers and fix Toddler Dinners and wash clothes and stay in a tiny cabin with a baby for three months straight.

"But I can't handle ringing telephones and dolls with staring blue eyes that are ripped and slashed and broken. I can't handle jealous husbands and odd questions and ringing telephones. Especially ringing telephones!"

"You mentioned that three times," Mrs. Nelson said, calmly making tea.

Her calmness made Becky feel even more frantic.

"I quit!" she repeated.

"Sit down and have some tea," Mrs. Nelson ordered.

Surprised, Becky sat.

"You're stronger than you think," Mrs. Nelson said. "We all are. We never think we can do things until we find ourselves doing them. Devon needs your help. You won't run out on him until you're sure he's safe."

Becky sighed, recognizing the truth. Her temper evaporated.

"I saw Franklin. He's on his way," Mrs. Nelson said.

Chapter 31

"What?" Becky leapt to her feet, ready to grab the baby and run. "Where is he? Who told you? Why are we sitting here?"

"He was on the ferry. He had his car. He's waiting for a tire to be fixed."

Mrs. Nelson smiled grimly, and Becky knew she had arranged to have the tire flattened.

"He had to hire someone with a boat to take him to Friday Harbor," Mrs. Nelson went on. "The tire was pretty well destroyed, so he had to get a new one. Actually, two tires were destroyed, but he had a spare so he only needed to buy one. Anyway, the tire will be in soon, and it won't take long to put it on the car. I thought we needed a cup of tea before we did anything, but I think now it's time to gather Devon's things. I wish I could take everything . . . his things are so cute. I got to pick them out myself. Franklin chose everything before, you know."

Becky couldn't remember ever feeling so flustered. "What do I do first?" she asked. "What do you want packed?"

"Everything that you can fit in this bag," Mrs. Nelson said, handing her a small traveling bag. "Whatever you think he'll need. Be sure to pack his bunny rabbit outfit, and those blue corduroy slacks. Socks to match, of course. Whatever you think. I've got most of my own things packed. Can you carry all that at once? My suitcase, his bag, and the baby?"

Oh, no! Becky thought. An important detail we didn't think of! How can I carry all that? I can't. She ran off to pack Devon's clothes. She grabbed outfits, socks, and sweaters, glad she had just done the laundry so everything was neat, clean, and handy.

She stuffed Devon's teddy bear in the bag, and pajamas, fresh diapers, spare plastic pants. She ran to the kitchen and grabbed his bottles of juice, tossed in extra nipples, and fixed one bottle of milk. She threw in crackers and apples, Cheerios, and jars of Toddler Dinner, adding sweet potatoes and ignoring the peas. She tossed his little spoons in the bag, and some bibs. The warming tray wouldn't fit, so she left it behind, zipped the bag shut, and tossed it by the back door. She gathered blankets, folding them over the bag.

Is that it? Does he need anything else? Becky eyed the bag critically, thinking. He can get by for two or three days, she decided. After that, his mom can buy him whatever he needs. After that, he'll be safe . . . and I'll never see him again.

She wiped at the tears that had started falling.

"Here." Mrs. Nelson handed Becky an enormous suitcase and a smaller bag. "I hope I'll be able to send for the rest of the things," Mrs. Nelson said, looking sad. "I packed my very favorites, but I hate to leave any of it behind. One never knows about vandals. It might not be safe here with us gone."

It must be her way of coping, Becky decided, setting the suitcases outside the back door. If she thinks about her clothes, she won't have to think about the rest of it.

"I probably won't be able to carry it all," Becky said. "I'll have to leave some of it. It'll be hidden behind the first tree on the route. You can bring it when you come."

Mrs. Nelson didn't argue, but she compressed her lips, looking angry.

Because she might have to carry a suitcase? Becky thought.

"I wish this weren't happening," Mrs. Nelson said.

Becky nodded. That's why she's angry, she told herself. Not about the suitcase. It's the whole mess.

"Now we wait," Mrs. Nelson said, moving to the window where the road was visible down the hill. "He has to come that way. And we'll see him."

I could go ahead, Becky thought, pacing nervously. I could grab Devon and get out of here now. I don't want to see that man. I just want to go!

But she knew if she left, their half-hour timed interval would be impossible to match. She and Mrs.

Nelson had to start timing at the same minute. They didn't want to leave Devon alone any longer than necessary.

I could carry the suitcases there and then come back, Becky thought. But she knew that wasn't a good idea, either. Mr. Nelson might come while she was gone.

She just wanted to be doing something . . . anything except waiting for a madman to show up and hurt them.

He won't hurt us, Becky told herself.

But she didn't believe it.

He's going to be angry. Hurt and angry. He'll want his son, and Devon won't be here. All the time, all the work, all the money he probably spent tracking Devon down, and he'll be gone.

Mr. Nelson will be angry.

"I see the headlights," Mrs. Nelson said, and Becky ran.

Chapter 32

Devon woke up, but only looked around sleepily. He made some tired noises that sounded like questions, and Becky hushed him, trying to sound reassuring.

The woods were choked with trees. Becky dropped her boss's suitcases behind the first fir on the way to the playpen and got a better grip on Devon, almost crying out at the ghostly shadows the moon sent creeping across his face as she ran through the trees.

The woods were full of noises made by unseen creatures. The trees trembled above her, and Becky felt as if her mind were spinning in an uncontrolled whirl. Panicked thoughts scrabbled in her brain, making a frenzied clawing, demanding to be heard.

No! Becky told them. Don't bother me. I can't panic now.

But the thoughts wormed their way to the surface. Behind her Becky heard shouting. Mr. Nelson had arrived.

"You've gone too far, Patricia!" he shouted. "You aren't going to get away with this! I want my son!"

Becky ran on, stumbling from Devon's sleepy weight and the awkward banging of his bag against her hip, thunk, thunk.

Footsteps? Becky thought, whirling. No. No one is here. She stumbled again and made herself slow her pace.

I don't want to drop him.

Against her will, images popped into her mind. Mrs. Nelson's pale face . . . Cleve, looking rugged and mischievous, his smile lighting up his face . . . the suspicious distance that replaced the warmth and turned him into a stranger.

Too much has happened, Becky thought, reliving the tumble into the chilly water and her fear that the whales were going to swallow her.

I don't know what any of it means. I didn't have time to think. Maybe this island makes people weird. Cleve asked some pretty strange questions . . . but maybe it was just me. Maybe I just caught Mrs. Nelson's tensions and everything looked suspicious.

But . . . she stopped running, the thoughts scrambling around furiously, erupting in images and questions.

Something doesn't add up.

Cleve or the sheriff or Mr. Nelson or John Hillyer. Something doesn't add up.

I don't have the whole truth here.

Becky leaned against a tree, holding Devon

tightly. He had his arms around her neck, his head trustingly cradled against her.

He expects me to make the right decision, Becky thought grimly. I have to think.

It's time for me to quit reacting blindly, and do something that makes sense. It's up to me.

Chapter 33

Becky made her way back to the cabin, walking quickly but quietly in the moonlight, wondering if she'd made the right decision. She had made a change in the plan. Someone will be angry with me, she thought. But I had to do something that made sense to me.

I just didn't have enough time to think. I had to trust someone. Who better than myself?

She hadn't noticed whether Mrs. Nelson's suitcases were still by the tree, but it was almost precisely thirty minutes since she'd left, so perhaps they'd passed in the forest, both being so quiet they hadn't heard each other.

The lights of the cabin shone softly through the shades and curtains, illuminating the back clearing with an eerie glow. Becky stepped onto the porch and reached for the doorknob, hoping she'd been right.

If I was wrong, I've messed everything up. I

didn't have enough information, she thought. I needed more. . . .

There was a slight rustling to her left, but before Becky could whirl around her head exploded in a Fourth of July spectacular that was too near, too blinding, too . . .

. . . too painful to be beautiful. And it isn't even the Fourth, she thought vaguely.

Smell. Funny smell. Where am I?

She tried to sit up, but her body parts weren't responding. For a second she knew they'd been ripped from her like they'd been ripped from the doll, and she started to cry.

My arms, she thought sadly. My arms are gone.

She moved one arm and it flopped loosely, then came up and touched her head.

Oh. My arms are here.

It smells.

Wasn't I outside?

Her brain felt foggy, but she was sure she'd been outside, walking home from Sarah's . . . no. Sarah stole Jason. I wasn't at her house. Not anymore. Then where?

Gas!

As she recognized the smell, she remembered everything . . . up to the fireworks in her head.

Someone hit me. Mr. Nelson?

She struggled to her feet, fighting waves of nausea. Her head felt as if it had split open, the ache fierce. If it hadn't been for the smell of gas, she would have lain back down and gone to sleep.

Something told her she was in the cabin. In the living room, she thought. She nodded once to agree with her assessment, but the throbbing in her head worsened sharply.

Okay, she thought. I'll do it without moving my head.

Do what?

She knew she'd thought of something she had to do, something that had driven her to her feet in spite of the pain and nausea. But she couldn't think what it was.

The smell of gas was making her head hurt worse.

Gas! That's it. I have to turn the gas off.

It was dark in the cabin, darker than she could remember it ever being.

There were lights when I came. She remembered the lights shining eerily from the windows. Like a warning, she thought. And I didn't pay attention.

I need a light. I can't see. No . . . electricity sparks. Turning things on can . . . do what? Make a spark. Make the gas explode.

She touched her head again, dizzy, trying to orient herself. Finally she realized there was a faint light from the moon shining on a window, and the window was in the front wall, therefore . . . she set off in the direction opposite the window, toward the kitchen, and stumbled over a dead body, falling hard.

She screamed.

The dead body moaned.

Chapter 34

No, they don't moan if they're dead, she thought numbly.

Who is it?

She realized the gas smell was getting stronger and she knew if she didn't get it turned off, the dead body would really be dead, and so would she. She clambered over the undead unknown person, crawling toward the kitchen, finally regaining her feet. She held her hands out in front of her, feeling blind and sick and hurt, feeling also for furniture and obstacles and other bodies.

She reached the stove by feel. The smell was overpowering, and she retched, fumbling for the knobs. She didn't find them. Frantic, she ran her hands over the stove again, sobbing. The knobs were gone. Someone had removed them. There was no way to turn the stove off.

She felt along the wall and pulled the back door open, running outside and gulping air. It was the sweetest thing she'd ever tasted, and she stood, breathing, feeling like a millionaire until she remembered the undead person dying inside the cabin. Dying of gas poisoning.

Who is it? John Hillyer? Mrs. Nelson? Mr. Nelson? Someone else entirely? Who cares? Get away from here. Run!

But instead of running, she took a deep breath and dashed back into the kitchen, her brain feeling more scrambled with each thumping step. She held her hands in front of her again, skimming the table as she hurried around it, feeling for the chairs. She tried to make it to the living room before she took a breath of gas-filled air, but in spite of her care she kicked something in the dark and fell again, hard, gasping, breathing the gas.

Get out! her brain said. Save yourself. You don't know who it is in there, and you've done the best you can. You're poisoning yourself. Breathing this air is poison.

Open the windows?

No time. Just get out. It's going to kill you. If the gas doesn't kill you, the explosion will. Gas explodes.

Her heart hammered, and she felt as if she were choking to death. She was so dizzy she felt as if she were on some kind of madly whirling amusement park ride, and her stomach had started making queasy complaints. Her chest hurt. Her head hurt.

She got to her knees again.

Doesn't gas settle? Isn't it heavier near the floor? Get up, Becky. Get up, or die right here.

She felt as if she were moving underwater again, with the heavy jeans and shoes weighing her down, pulling her under. She forced herself to her feet and held onto the doorway for a moment, swaying.

Where is the body? In front of me? Or behind? I found it once. I never was any good at hide-and-seek. Can't find a good hiding place and everyone else can. Where is it? Don't hide from me. Not now.

She stumbled, coughing, feeling her way blindly and found the undead person by stumbling over it once again. She had no time to wonder who it was. She could tell she was fading. All she wanted to do was sleep, or throw up, but she grabbed two large feet . . . not Mrs. Nelson . . . who, then? . . . tugging, pulling, her lungs must be turned inside out . . . they felt raw, bleeding.

She pulled until she started to sway, almost fainting. Then she ran outside again, breathing deeply of the pure night air.

Going back inside the cabin was like stepping into the jaws of a killer whale, stepping into the black depths of death.

This time she grabbed the body under the arms and tried to run out the door with it, bent in an awkward stoop, running in glue, her feet stuck, her body screaming in protest, her mind split like a fork in the road with half commanding her to run outside and live, half dimly but unbendingly committed to getting the body outside.

It was a heavy body, flopping . . . dead? Or undead?

It didn't matter. She wouldn't let go now.

I am the rescuer. Wading pools and gas-filled cabins.

And finally, after forever of being stuck in the glue and stuck in the dark, sharp agony, she burst through the door to the heavenly outside with pure air and wept with the pleasure of breathing.

She breathed and breathed, tears of joy streaming down her face. I made it!

But she hadn't made it, and slowly the realization dawned that the cabin could still explode. The gas smell was still strong, even outside. The inside was a bomb, just waiting for its flashpoint.

Gasping, Becky bent and grabbed the body again, tugging and hauling it over the rocky clearing, through the softly needled, spongy ground at the edge of the firs and into the forest, hauling the possibly dead, hopefully undead, unknown man . . . it was a man, hauling him from the time bomb, farther, farther, not far enough.

The world exploded again, the fireworks bigger, louder, so bright that she knew if she weren't fainting, she would be blinded.

Chapter 35

This time she woke even more slowly, the noise and lights battering unendingly against her senses.

"Are you there?" someone kept asking, and Becky wished they would stop. Just shut up, she thought. Leave me alone. You're too loud.

"One-niner, is Joe there? Give me Joe."

I don't know any Joes, Becky thought. Go find him if you want him. Just quit yelling at me.

"Are you okay? Becky?"

Finally she realized it was Cleve, but nothing seemed to make sense beyond that realization. It hurt when she opened her eyes. It hurt when she breathed. It hurt if she kept her eyes closed and didn't breathe.

"She moved!" Cleve called, and then people were talking to her.

She didn't want to answer. Answering meant thinking, and thinking meant remembering, and remembering meant . . .

"Go away," she muttered, squeezing her eyes shut.

She heard a soft chuckle. "We can't do that," a voice said calmly. "We're fighting a fire here and we have to stay till it's out. Can you tell me your name?"

She didn't want to speak, but if speaking would make the noise stop . . . "Becky," she said. Her tongue felt dry, and her chest still hurt.

Still hurt? It hurt before?

Again, the memories swept back into her brain. "Was he dead or undead?" she asked.

"Undead," Cleve said. "It was Mr. Nelson you saved, Becky. He said his ex-wife has been hiding out here with his child. He's been trying to telephone for days. When he finally got here, she bashed him in the head. You saved him. The cabin exploded."

"It was her child, too," Becky protested, her eyes still squeezed shut against the light.

"No," Cleve said softly. "Mr. Nelson divorced her almost eight years ago. Devon belongs to him and his second wife."

Becky digested the information slowly.

"Where is the baby?" she asked. "I changed Mrs. Nelson's plan. I took Devon to your house!"

"He's here," Cleve said. "He's with his father right now. I'm never baby-sitting for you again, by the way. Little kids don't like me. He cried until I gave him a candy bar . . . "

"You what?" Becky struggled to sit up, but Cleve pushed her back down.

"Don't move yet," he said. "We're pretty sure you have a concussion at least. I know the candy was a bad idea, only I'd do it again. It shut him up."

Becky was silent for a moment, thinking. If Mrs. Nelson wasn't the mother . . . I was aiding a kidnapper! "Where is Mrs. Nelson?" she asked.

"We don't know," Cleve said. "No one's seen her. We've been in touch with Calvin, and he's ordered some backups. When they get here, they'll search."

She'll be gone, Becky thought. "She'll be gone," she said. "We've got to go get her."

"No." Cleve's voice was firm against the background noise of the firefighting. "You're not going anywhere. Especially not looking for her. Mr. Nelson said quite a bit about her, Becky, and she's dangerous. Who do you think smashed in the back of your head? She told Mr. Nelson he was going to die, and she told him he'd have company. He thought she meant Devon, but I guess she meant you. She left you both to die. She knew the cabin would explode! She planned it."

It wasn't her baby! Becky thought, slowly putting things together. No wonder she didn't know how to take care of him. No wonder she was so calm about our plans. She knew what she was going to do. Kill me. She was going to kill me!

"Cleve, we could use you over here."

Cleve glanced toward the voice, then back. "I'm

firefighting," he told Becky. "Joe's unit isn't here. He's bringing a chopper, but they haven't been able to get him on radio yet so they need my help. Will you be okay? I'll send the medic over to check you again as soon as he's got Mr. Nelson fixed up."

"I'm fine," Becky said.

"You're not even remotely fine," Cleve said, giving her his mischievous grin. "But you will be. I bandaged your head. I made sure nothing was broken. I made all kinds of wild promises if you'd just wake up and now that you did wake up, I guess I'll have to keep them. But first you lie still, and I'll go help with the fire. Don't move. Promise?"

But we've got to find Mrs. Nelson, Becky thought.

"Don't go after her!" Cleve said sternly, reading her eyes. "Promise me."

She got me into this, Becky thought. She hired me, lied to me, kidnapped a child and made me part of it, then tried to kill me. She isn't going to get away.

"Becky," Cleve said. "I mean it. I'll tie you to a tree if I have to. You've got a concussion. She's dangerous."

Becky let her eyes flutter shut. She groaned weakly. "My head hurts," she said.

"I know. Here . . . use this." Cleve took off his jacket and rolled it up. "Can you lift your head?"

"Maybe," Becky said, struggling to sit up. "Why does it hurt to breathe?"

"Gas," Cleve said, reverting to his one-word answers.

"Cleve!" the voice called. It held a note of exhaustion and impatience.

"Coming." Cleve slipped the jacket under Becky's head and kissed her quickly. "I'll be back," he promised. "You just wait."

"I will wait," Becky told him. I will wait as long as I need to, she added silently. I think you're pretty special, Cleve Davidson, and I'm not letting you get away.

But I'm not going to wait by lying here while Mrs. Nelson escapes. I'm going to find her.

She rolled to her side and sat up slowly, waiting for the nausea to subside, then lurched to her feet.

I think I know where she is. I think she told me a little bit of the truth — about arranging for a ride — and I can find her.

She swayed, but reached out and held onto a tree trunk until she felt steadier, then slipped quietly into the woods, stumbling from tree to tree for support as she headed for the path to the point.

Chapter 36

As she moved through the woods, she heard the shouts of the firefighters carrying through the shadows like a bad dream. The night hissed and crackled eerily, and charred timbers crashed behind her as they fell. The smell of smoke and of drowned ashes wafted through the air. The sky behind her was lit by flames, in front of her the path was lit by the moon.

Gradually she felt a little stronger, but the dizziness persisted. She had to sit periodically and wait for the spells to pass, then struggle to her feet again and go on.

Her mind still worked oddly, one moment her thoughts seeming clear and logical, the next moment fuzzy and incoherent.

I knew it wasn't Cleve, she thought. At the end. Only it hasn't ended yet. Mrs. Nelson told me she made sure no one knew that her husband had smashed her dolls. And never let her husband see how upset losing her dolls made her. If he didn't know, how could he use dolls as a threat?

Mrs. Nelson was the only one who knew. So only she could have been slashing them and putting them around. She came back that day. What day? Was it today? Earlier today? Yesterday? It doesn't matter. She came back and gave Devon the doll. She plugged the phone back in and left the door unlocked. Only she could have done it. So it wasn't Cleve.

She lied. She lied about everything. And I helped. She lured me here. She used me. She used me to hurt Devon! I love Devon. I love Cleve, too. Not Mrs. Nelson. I don't love her. Why am I climbing up? In all the movies, they always climb up. And then they get stuck up high with no way to get down.

But she went up. To the point. Babyface.

She shuddered, remembering the climb down. It had seemed scary enough in the daytime. The shudder set up a protest in her body, and she had to sit again while the pain in her head and chest slowed enough that she could go on.

How long has it been? Mrs. Nelson could be gone by now.

The path was covered with humus, and her footsteps made only the tiniest thumping, yet even that reverberated in her head, aching, pounding with the ache, rhythmic and dull.

The path split, and Becky realized she was near the point. She remembered the trees crowding close on the right, so she kept right, hiding in the trees, wanting to see Mrs. Nelson first, before Mrs. Nelson saw her . . . and attacked her.

I need something, Becky thought. A weapon would be nice.

She felt around on the forest floor, discarding the little twigs she kept finding, trying to pick up a stick that looked just right . . . except it was still connected to a fallen tree.

Can't carry the whole tree, she told herself.

Finally she stopped again, listening.

"Hush little baby, don't say a word. Mama's going to buy you a mockingbird. I said hush. Stop that crying this instant!"

Becky peered through the trees.

Mrs. Nelson was sitting, holding a doll. The same doll — or its twin, that Becky had kicked under Devon's crib.

She was sitting in a shaft of moonlight, cradling the unbroken, unslashed doll. She still had on a dress, and her hair was perfectly smooth. She looked ready for a day at the office except for the smudge of dirt on her cheek.

She was crying, her tears smearing the smudge, trickling in little dark streaks down to her chin.

She looks like a little girl playing grownup, Becky thought sadly.

Though she'd have sworn she hadn't made a noise, as she watched, Mrs. Nelson suddenly looked up, right at her.

Can she see me through the trees?

"What do you want?" Mrs. Nelson asked. "It's rude to eavesdrop. At least have the courtesy of showing your face."

Becky swallowed, but she needed to confront the woman. That's what she'd come here for. She stepped from the trees, feeling exposed. Keep your back to the trees, she reminded herself. Don't get near the edge.

"Oh, it's you," Mrs. Nelson said. "I didn't leave your check. How thoughtless of me, making you come all this way to get it."

She reached beside her and picked up her purse, rummaged inside, and withdrew a checkbook. She wrote, tore the check out, and tossed it to Becky. It fluttered, falling to her feet.

Becky glanced down at it, and at that moment Mrs. Nelson leapt at her, a huge knotted stick in her hands.

She had it beside her, Becky thought. In the shadows.

"You took my baby!" Mrs. Nelson shrieked, slashing at Becky with the stick.

Becky jumped back, the sudden terror making her forget her head wound. She landed and stumbled, the dizziness washing over her again. Mrs. Nelson was on her in a second, but she'd dropped the stick and was only slapping Becky's face and pulling her hair.

Like a playground fight, Becky thought dumbly, twisting to avoid the slaps. Each blow rocked her head, setting up a clamor inside like a traffic accident, crashing, horns blaring, the shriek of metal on metal.

"He . . . wasn't . . . yours," Becky said, trying to make her hands work fast enough to grab Mrs. Nelson's. "You took him from his father. You stole him. I only gave him back."

"He should have been mine," Mrs. Nelson snapped, but she stopped slapping long enough for Becky to grab her wrists and cross them tightly in front of her.

"I didn't mean all those things," Mrs. Nelson went on, her face angry. "I didn't mean to burn the books and things, but he wouldn't forgive. Why should he care about an old tuxedo?"

She did it all, Becky thought sadly. All the things she said Mr. Nelson did, she did. She burned the yearbooks, burned his tuxedo. She shivered, then realized a mist had blown in, obscuring the moon. I'm cold, Becky thought. Cold and sore.

Mrs. Nelson's face grew still, thoughtful. Her dress was slightly rumpled, but her hair was still in place. She looked as if she could have been sitting at home, thinking about the evening's menu instead of caught in the middle of a fight in the forest.

But her face is dirty, Becky thought, waiting. As long as Mrs. Nelson wasn't moving, Becky didn't move either. She didn't have the strength.

She'd be embarrassed if she knew her face was dirty, Becky thought.

"Well." Mrs. Nelson snatched her hands easily

from Becky's grip. "I guess you wouldn't die, either, if I threw you over the cliff. The sheriff didn't. You probably wouldn't. I thought the gas would work. What else can I use?"

Fear crept through Becky like a damp chill, starting in her stomach, working its way to her chest, making it even harder to breathe. She tried to kill Calvin, then me and Mr. Nelson.

"It didn't work," Becky said. Her voice sounded like a squeak. "You aren't supposed to kill us."

Exasperated, Mrs. Nelson asked, "What else can I do? You just don't understand. It all worked so beautifully till now. I have to get you out of the way. You're not out of the way."

"I will be," Becky said. "I'll take a ferry and go home."

"No, you're just lying to me. I suppose that's okay. I lied to you."

"You're lost," Becky said, thinking out loud. "Lost in your mind. You don't live in the same world I do. I was right. You don't have the same built-in stopping points other people do. I couldn't have taken Devon from his parents. I just couldn't have done it. You didn't have a problem doing it."

"What do you know about problems?" Mrs. Nelson asked, her face almost sneering. "I had nothing but problems. Everyone else could do the right things without thinking, but I would think and think and still do the wrong thing. I always said the wrong thing. I was never just . . . " Her face crumpled.

"I was never just plain normal. All I wanted was

to be normal. Everybody looked at me. They whispered behind my back. I had *problems*. I had to go to special schools. I was never invited. Never invited anywhere. All I wanted was to go to the prom with a nice boy. I wanted a boyfriend . . . a husband, and a job, and a baby. I wanted to be NORMAL! I wanted someone to love me, even with my problems. Is that so much to ask?"

It's all anyone wants, Becky thought. She suddenly felt like weeping. We only want to belong. We only want to be loved. She was still lying on the ground beneath Mrs. Nelson, and she watched as the woman's face disintegrated, falling into despair. Mrs. Nelson sobbed, covering her face. Her shoulders shook, and her weeping sounded desolate. Becky knew she was hearing the sound of absolute sadness and loneliness and hopelessness.

Behind them a horn blared . . . not the foghorn sound of the ferry, but a boat horn nonetheless . . . and not far away.

"Is that your ride?" Becky asked softly.

Mrs. Nelson looked at her, her face suddenly hopeful. "You'll let me go?"

You're the one who has me pinned to the ground, Becky thought. But she didn't point that out. "Yes," she said. "Go quickly. Go far away with your friend. And be safe."

She hurt us, Becky thought. But she didn't hurt us forever. We'll mend. She won't. I could try to hold her here and turn her in. But why? They'd only put her away, and no matter where she is, she has to live with herself. She'll either destroy what's there, or she'll let it mend. It's up to her, not me.

Mrs. Nelson scrambled off of her, and Becky could suddenly breathe again. She took several deep breaths, watching as Mrs. Nelson hurried toward the point, looking back over her shoulder as if expecting Becky to leap up and stop her.

Then the woman turned and started the climb down Boniface, down the same cliff she'd pushed the sheriff over, down Babyface, the beginner's climb, down to whatever freedom and normalcy she could make of her life . . . until and unless they caught her, or until and unless she pushed herself over the edge.

Becky stood. She crept to the edge of the point. The mist had grown stronger below her, becoming a fog across the ocean. Becky peered over the side but she couldn't see Mrs. Nelson, even though the woman couldn't have gotten far yet. She had simply vanished in the mist. Becky sighed.

The walk to the point and the fight with Mrs. Nelson hadn't done her head any good. Becky could feel warmth oozing through the bandage and down her neck. She sighed again and ignored the blood. It didn't seem important.

I couldn't rescue her, Becky thought, bending to pick up her check. I could rescue someone from a pool — if I didn't have my jeans and shoes on and if killer whales weren't looking over my shoulder with their mouths open. But this is different. Can anyone rescue someone from themselves?

She looked at the check and laughed, even though it hurt her head.

The check was for $5,000.00, made out to Rebecca Collier, signed by Rebecca Collier.

Chapter 37

"I can't help wondering if she got away," Cleve said.

"I think she did," Becky told him. "They never found her suitcases. Someone had to come after them."

"She could have put them on one of the ledges earlier," Cleve pointed out. "Maybe she stumbled on them. She could have knocked them into the sea and fallen after them. They might never find the body. The ocean is pretty big."

"I don't care. I still think she got away." Becky shifted positions, trying to get comfortable. "What do you mean it was your cabin?" she demanded.

Cleve handed her a glass of iced tea and adjusted the pillow behind her head. He sat in the lounge chair next to hers. "Don't get too used to being waited on," he warned. "It's my turn next. Fair's fair."

"If you get smashed on the head two times, I'll wait on you for awhile, too," Becky promised, grinning. "What do you mean it was your cabin?"

"It was my uncle's," Cleve said. "He died. I inherited. I'm rich, you know."

"So am I," Becky said smugly. "Mr. Nelson paid me. He gave me extra as a reward for rescuing Devon. You still haven't explained about your cabin."

"We always rented it to John Hillyer, so when I found you and your 'aunt' there, I couldn't figure out what was going on. John was living in a little apartment in town, and you two were here. I didn't want to seem too suspicious of you, especially since I kind of liked you right from the start. So I asked a few innocent questions. . . . "

"Hah! Innocent? You were so bizarre I thought you were nuts."

"Well . . . okay. I asked a few weird questions. So I wasn't thinking at my best. I already graduated. I don't have to think anymore. Besides, you were incredibly distracting. Anyway, John finally admitted he'd rented it to Becky Collier — that's you, by the way, or so you said. I didn't know what to think. John had sublet the cabin, with a contract and all, making a nice profit. The problem was, he described Mrs. Nelson, but it was your name on the contract.

"I was curious. Who wouldn't be? Something funny was going on, and I just wanted to know what. Especially since it was going on in my cabin, which made me legally responsible. If a crime is committed in my cabin, or if there's an accident or something, I'm the one who gets sued. I'm a little miffed, though, that you thought I might be a doll-slasher. I can understand you thinking I was a little strange, but a doll-slasher?"

"I trusted you when it mattered," Becky said in defense. "I took Devon to you."

Cleve laughed. "Don't ever do it again, please! Babies and I do not get along."

"Did you sing to him?" Becky asked.

"No."

"Did you rock him? Pace the floor? Tell him soothing things?"

"No."

"Next summer I'll teach you how to do all of those things, and you and Devon will learn to like each other," Becky said. "Mr. Nelson already hired me for the whole summer. I get to stay at their place, with a swimming pool and horses. I don't have to do any housework or cooking, just baby-sit. And I get every night off after Devon's asleep."

"Is that an invitation?" Cleve asked, leaning over to kiss her.

Becky put her arms around his neck. "Watch the head," she said. "It's not back to normal." The word resonated in her mind, and she felt a pang of sympathy for Mrs. Nelson. The matter was still unresolved, but it looked as if no one would be looking for her . . . at least not because of this episode. She was missing, presumed far away or dead.

"It's more than an invitation," Becky murmured to Cleve. "It's an order. I want you there every night to rescue me from the terrible two-year-old.

He'll be two next summer, you know. And they really are terrible."

What are?" Cleve asked, kissing her gently.

"Boys," Becky said. "Boys are terrible. No matter what age." She kissed him back, and her thoughts turned briefly to Jason and Sarah.

Good luck, she thought, and she wasn't sure if it was Jason or Sarah she was wishing luck. Or perhaps Mrs. Nelson.

It didn't matter, she wished them all luck.

GREEN WATCH by Anthony Masters

BATTLE FOR THE BADGERS
Tim's been sent to stay with his weird Uncle Seb and his
two kids, Flower and Brian, who run Green Watch – an
environmental pressure group. At first Tim thinks they're
a bunch of cranks – but soon he finds himself battling to
save badgers from extermination . . .

SAD SONG OF THE WHALE
Tim leaps at the chance to join Green Watch on an anti-
whaling expedition. But soon, he and the other members of
Green Watch, find themselves shipwrecked and fighting
for their lives . . .

DOLPHIN'S REVENGE
The members of Green Watch are convinced that Sam
Jefferson is mistreating his dolphins – but how can they
prove it? Not only that, but they must save Loner, a wild
dolphin, from captivity . . .

MONSTERS ON THE BEACH
The Green Watch team is called to investigate a suspected
radiation leak. Teddy McCormack claims to have seen
mutated crabs and sea-plants, but there's no proof, and
Green Watch don't know whether he's crazy or there's
been a cover-up . . .

GORILLA MOUNTAIN
Tim, Brian and Flower fly to Africa to meet the Bests, who
are protecting gorillas from poachers. But they are
ambushed and Alison Best is kidnapped. It is up to them to
rescue her *and* save the gorillas . . .

SPIRIT OF THE CONDOR
Green Watch has gone to California on a surfing holiday –
but not for long! Someone is trying to kill the Californian
Condor, the bird cherished by an Indian tribe – the Daiku
– without which the tribe will die. Green Watch must
struggle to save both the Condor and the Daiku . . .

THE BABYSITTERS CLUB

Need a babysitter? Then call the Babysitters Club. Kristy Thomas and her friends are all experienced sitters. They can tackle any job from rampaging toddlers to a pandemonium of pets. To find out all about them, read on!

The Babysitters Club No 1:
Kristy's Great Idea
The Babysitters Club No 2:
Claudia and the Phantom Phone Calls
The Babysitters Club No 3:
The Truth About Stacey
The Babysitters Club No 4:
Mary Anne Saves The Day
The Babysitters Club No 5:
Dawn and the Impossible Three
The Babysitters Club No 6:
Kristy's Big Day
The Babysitters Club No 7:
Claudia and Mean Janine
The Babysitters Club No 8:
Boy Crazy Stacey
The Babysitters Club No 9:
The Ghost at Dawn's House
The Babysitters Club No 10:
Logan Likes Mary Anne!
The Babysitters Club No 11:
Kristy and the Snobs
The Babysitters Club No 12:
Claudia and the New Girl
The Babysitters Club No 13:
Goodbye, Stacey, Goodbye
The Babysitters Club No 14:
Hello, Mallory

Look out for:

The Babysitters Club No 15:
Little Miss Stoneybrook . . . and Dawn
The Babysitters Club No 16:
Jessi's Secret Language
The Babysitters Club No 17:
Mary Anne's Bad Luck Mystery
The Babysitters Club No 18:
Stacey's Mistake
The Babysitters Club No 19:
Claudia and the Bad Joke
The Babysitters Club No 20:
Kristy and the Walking Disaster
The Babysitters Club No 21:
Mallory and the Trouble with Twins
The Babysitters Club No 22:
Jessi Ramsey, Pet-sitter
The Babysitters Club No 23:
Dawn on the Coast
The Babysitters Club No 24:
Kristy and the Mother's Day Surprise